Danny

WINTERLAND

best wishes. let's catch
some fish!

Rob Conery

Cover photo: "Winterland"

Author photo by Lynne Perera

Praise for *Winterland*:

"For Conery's wildcat characters, the road to Winterland is steep and deep—a carved up mogul run of money and drugs, big deals, bad decisions, high stakes and higher times."

—*Charles Graeber, New York Times bestselling author of The Good Nurse*

"Winterland is a no-holds-barred tale of a young man who stops at nothing to save a small ski town from falling into the hands of corporate America. If you've ever lived in a ski town this is a must read."

—*Todd Jones, filmmaker, Teton Gravity Research*

"Conery's descriptive style is energetic and truthful. The Author's take on who we are and how we behave sneaks up on us and makes an impact… the story unfolds masterfully; I was unable to stop reading. Incredible twists and turns in this Bright, Funny and Brilliant novel."

—*John Ennis, actor, Mr. Show*

A Strawberry Book

www.strawberrybooks.com

IMAGINE

Strawberry Books is a publishing house that thrills, delights and informs our readers with high-quality e-books, physical books and online content.

Please check out our website above and follow us on Twitter:

@thrillsdelights

Table of Contents

The Bonfire

Flames roared into the dark chasm of the cold Colorado night. Burning embers wafted over the crowd, casting shifting shadows across the faces of revelers.

It was almost time.

People crowded around, edged ever closer, eager for the spectacle. Thin guys in corduroy pants and hiking boots held tele boards, a bearded guy with no shirt stood ready with yellow Kastles. A pretty girl in an oversize wool sweater held a single K2 and smiled beatifically.

The Florida-LSU game progressed in the house, unwatched. On the deck, the DJ stopped blasting funk. The roast, savagely butchered into sloppy, greasy piles of charred pig slabs lay forgotten on the picnic table, surrounded now only by a dozen patient dogs. Even the line at the keg had thinned to a trickle. It was almost time.

The flames roared higher. More wood was heaved into the maw. Firewood mixed with construction scraps and PBR twelvers for fuel. Finally, whole pallets were kicked into the breach. The heat grew intense. A lone figure burst from the crowd and ran towards the fire. He tried to use the remaining pallets as a backwoods springboard. He timed his leap and sprang forward, directly into the wall of flame. He barely made it. He was half dragged out the other side, his smoldering pants doused with beers from friendly strangers. Eyes danced on his cherubic face. He laughed like a loon.

No one would try that again. It was almost time.

Pagans danced in wild anticipation around the fire, personifying powder prayers. With a scream a guy raised skis over his head like an Olympic power lifter, paused, and flung last year's boards towards this year's hope. That's all it took. Skis rained in from the darkness, landing in twisting tumbles on the fire. The crowd roared and danced, the flames leapt higher. The lifts opened the next day.

It was time.

Part One
Ruined in a Day

Chapter One

On his last night on the island, Easy Ed struck it rich. Now, rich was a relative term in the late nineties, when dot.com millionaires were being pumped out of Silicon Valley like frogs. Rich also meant something new and very different to Ed, a flat-busted former trust fund kid with the funds now cut off. He'd been lashing about in the lower Keys, besotted, stumbling through rum soaked sunrises. Coasting on fumes long after the money had ran out. 86'd from this bar, an un-payable tab at another. But for a guy who'd sold his high school graduation present Jag convertible to buy a Corolla—then traded *that* to buy a case of Mt. Gay!—and currently drove an uninsured rust bucket, hey, it counted as rich.

That night, he decided to go fishing for the last time. He grabbed one of the community/beater kayaks from the dock by the marina and headed out into the mangroves, searching for tarpon breaking in the moonlight.

He was gliding silently, his stroke easy, the lights and chaos of Duval Street a few miles south. Key West—oh, fallen, fated beauty! Trading cheaply now on its outpost past, its icons reduced to plastic idolatry in the chintzy shops. A former art colony gone Disney, full of mild Rotarians benignly amused by the "street" performers—each just another licensed and taxed act in gray flannel pajamas working for the man. The open air bars full of post dream-death no hope chancers—fast talk and vague answers. No-more-options types who think that hitting rock bottom only means it's time to start drilling. Immediately to the north stood the ramshackle housing tracts of Stock Island, where the workers lived, hidden from view. End of the road.

Ed turned north, slid under a bridge on A1A and was soon in the vast maze of open flats and twisted clumps of dark mangrove islands that he had gotten to know. What had it been? Eight months? Ten? Too many rummy nights and squinty-eyed mornings on the water, his head throbbing as he watched some rich bozo make a bird's nest of his carefully tied tapered leader. Repeatedly.

The dull whoosh of traffic faded behind him. He headed deep into the mangroves. It was slack tide. When it turned the helpless bait would

3

begin to drift and the tarpon would strike quickly from the depths and shadows, looking for a shrimp dinner. It was still and quiet, his blades in the water making tiny splashes. Clouds hid the moon. His eyes adjusted to the light, he fell into a groove, paddling and then coasting, looking for telltale swirls on the calm surface. It was so dark that he didn't notice when he passed the guy standing chest deep in the water by the edge of a mangrove. A man's face that burned holes in him as he glided past, just a few feet to starboard. The face was intense, alert, unblinking and very, very dark. Ed never saw him. When he heard a splash astern, Ed shipped the paddle and reached for his fly rod, sure that a tarpon had just broken. But before he could turn, he was seized, his arms jerked behind him. A strong, gloved hand clamped over his mouth. A big light blinded him before he could see anything.

"Where's the load?"

"Where yo buddies at, man?"

"Where's the fucking drop, asshole!"

"Check him for weapons, sergeant."

What the fuck?

Ed saw men in black uniforms. Everywhere. They splashed chest deep in the water all around his kayak, stopping him.

"Where's the load?"

"Where the fuck is the load?"

The load? They kept asking him where the load was.

Ed had no idea what to say, not that he could speak with the powerfully gloved hand crushed tight over his grill. When the glove was removed, he gasped for breath.

"I'm looking for"—Boom! His face slammed into the kayak's bow, shoved and then held down from behind. He tasted plastic and rage and his own bile. They bent his arms up behind him— stress position number two—until he almost welcomed a break, if only to relieve the tension. Hot pain blinded him.

"—fish. I don't know about any load. I'm fishing!" He tried to shout, but he was out of breath and his face was smashed straight down into the kayak.

Ed felt something cold and hard in his ear. Too big. A gun!

"I'm going to ask you one more time, S.A., where the fuck are your buddies? Last chance, asshole." This last word hissed into his ear; stung. Hurt and shame and confusion.

"I'm *fishing*."

He didn't have his wallet on him, which complicated matters, but after about fifteen minutes of shoddy treatment and accusations, they were convinced he wasn't with the Calabras brothers and didn't know anything about tonight's offload. Their insignias branded them members of the Monroe County Drug Task Force and they were wired to the gills on adrenaline, jumpy and nervous, sure that they'd picked off a lookout or possibly a mule in the biggest drug sting in years. They had worked out on a lackey—seized during a routine traffic stop—and knew that this was the night.

"OK, motherfucker. If I was you, I'd make myself scarce about now. The vagaries of bullets in the night is legendary. Never know who might get hit. You hearing me, mutt? Get lost!"

Reluctantly they let Ed go. Then silently back in their black Zodiac inflatable and back into the night, still intent to kick some ass, they were gone.

Ed's heart beat in warm, wet thumps and it took many minutes for his breathing to return to normal. Now he sure every splash or dark form in the water was a spook ready to grab him, pull him under, down into the mire, until he could breath no more. Damn steroid freaks!

His fucking arms still hurt, too, where they'd bent them almost over his head from behind. He tried to look for tarpon boils, but all he could see was the demented, angry face of the guy who'd been questioning him. The sweat pouring through the camo grease paint, the bulge of foul Skoal in his lip. Fuckers. He wasn't gonna run home scared.

***

Oh, he'd had one hell of a run.

Once a promising tight end, he'd accepted a full ride from Carolina, spurning the opportunity to follow the old man, a paper and publishing magnate from Detroit, to Dartmouth like pops and the uncles and grandpa Ellsworth. No, he'd gone to Carolina on the full ride and made the old man begrudgingly proud, if only because he'd earned something on his own merit. An indifferent student, Ed had barely gotten in anyway—to land grant school! A *state* school! His father on the law review at Dartmouth!—and had to have the assistant coach pull a couple strings with admissions to make even that happen. His father had always stressed the importance of service, of giving back. The old noblese oblige, though he'd never use those words.

But there he was on that hot August day, running drills on the athletic fields by the big stadium, just a few months out of the Cranbrook

School in Bloomfield Hills. The season was looking good, nine starters back on offense from a team that played in the Gator Bowl on New Year's Day. Then he quit. He was gone before the first game of the season, content to sit in his dorm room and do blow with comely coeds. It was all so easy. The next party only a few hours away, the next gram just a phone call. Of course, he didn't tell the old man this. Ed knew he could coast on the scholarship for the rest of the semester. And worry about the rest of it later.

Well, the semester went by. Fast! Ed was immediately slapped on academic probation. His GPA ran a losing race against his blood alcohol content. Fuck, it had taken a last ditch effort to the tune of eight hundred bucks just to get some geek to write a term paper to get him that 'C' in US History Since 1865 that kept him from getting kicked out completely! And he'd had to go home at Christmas break and go upstairs to the oak paneled study to face the old man and tell him that things were going… Great! But that he wanted to focus on his studies for now, put football on the backburner, and could he please just write a check? Please?

And the old man did, and Easy Ed went back to Chapel Hill and helped a few drug dealers set new sales records in their district. And he stopped going to class all together, and he stopped pretending to be a college student at all times, except when speaking with the old man. Told the old man that he'd gotten a plum summer internship, that no, he wouldn't be home for summer break, but that things were…Great! And they were, in a way. He had an apartment near campus, and a car, and plenty of friends. Yep, it was a regular old college funfest, minus the college. And when August rolled around again, he'd convinced the old man just make the tuition check directly out to him, some complications between the registrar's office and the out of state bank, yeah, just make it out to me, thanks dad. And he got a check for nine thousand dollars and he kept the party going.

And then one day he came clean. In a flurry of coke-fueled truthfulness he asked his dad to release what was left in his trust so he could start over…somewhere. And the old man had hit the roof! Ed was cut off now, for good.

So with back rent due and owing money to the kind of brothers you don't want to owe money to, he'd ghosted Chapel Hill and drifted south. Ed headed down Florida. He lived on Stock Island, worked as a flats guide out of Key West and stopped doing drugs. Because of the piss tests. But the fishing was great. Tarpon the size of torpedoes! He was sick of drugs anyway, too many paranoid nights locked in his room with the lights out, jumping at threats in the shadows, sure that every sound was DEA crashing through the door. He didn't really do drugs in Key West. But at night, after a long day in the hot sun, the booze flowed in amber rivers. He stopped doing coke and he drank himself into irrelevance.

He worked as a mate on a fly fishing skiff. And it paid pretty well; on the days there was a charter, which were infrequent. Many times he'd be over at Hogfish, belly up to the bar by ten in the morning. But it was nice down here in the sun and the salt air and the warm water. The sky was close. The open space suited him fine.

And the ocean was magnificent. The deep cobalt out beyond the pale aqua and rumpled khaki of the flats that sparkled in the sun. And he'd gotten to love fly fishing, of all things.

Then he'd had one nice day out on the flats with a venture capitalist from New York, and they'd hit it off, talking football. They had gone for drinks after, and the guy had offered him a key bump. And they partied a little bit that night and went their separate ways.

Early the next morning the dock was crawling with Coast Guard, most of the charter fleet was piss tested and Ed was fired. Since his boss owned the trailer in which he was (barely) sleeping, he was suddenly unemployed and homeless. Ruined in a day. With the last "tuition" check long since spent and with no way to save money while paying twelve hundred a month, plus utilities, to rent half of a rusty trailer, he hadn't saved a dime. So he was headed home, tail between his legs, to throw himself on the mercy of the old man.

Stubby, his former captain/landlord/boss gave him twenty-four hours to scram. Ed's only cushion was the two hundred dollar security deposit he was owed. And even that again was no fucking guarantee. He'd gone out hard in that trailer. Fresh holes and stains marked the trajectory of his descent. He figured Stubby would try to screw him on the deposit. In fairness, even Ed would admit to causing *some* damage. Also, there had been an explosion…But still! Whatever the amount of his deposit, it was the only thing between him and oblivion. He hoped it would get him home. And how he hated the prospect of that.

***

Hector eased off the throttle, cast about for his marks. He'd made several dry runs. But it hadn't been this cloudy. He was ten minutes late now on the kind of job where timing was everything. Three days ago he'd been approached at the Green Parrot and asked if he was still in business. And he'd said no. He was retired now, living a quiet life on Key West.

7

He'd been a major player in the seventies, running bud from Columbia. But that was before the Cocaine Cowboys turned Miami into a shooting gallery. With blood in the streets, many of the old guard chose to get out while the getting was good. Like many of the former *contrabandistas*, he'd hung it up. Now he spent most days casting bait from the White Street pier and drinking café con leche.

But this job had been a layup. Just coordinate a drop, hook the couriers up with the product and that was it. Fifteen grand for three hours work. He'd barely have to touch the stuff; they just needed a local who knew the territory. And it was grass, not blow, and the money was right, so he said yes.

And now he regretted it. He was lost. He was sure he should have seen the little rope he'd tied to the branch indicating which channel in this fucking maze he was meant to turn left at, and now he was nervous. The crew grew tense as the minutes slipped away. He searched for the place to turn. And all he saw around him was dark and confusing.

***

Ed had hooked a tarpon, released it, and was on his way home when he saw the small skiff motor up the channel towards him. Shit, I've had enough cops for one night. But these weren't cops. While the cops were barely contained bundles of energy searching for a face to kick in, the desperation that gripped this boat was that of the hunted. Their boat looked like a salvage job; a fake Boston Whaler, beat to shit. Their little outboard gurgled along at idle speed as a shaky, handheld light scanned the dark water and tangled branches ahead of them. Ed sat very still on the edge of a mangrove. They were actually past him when they swung their light around and he heard a swear word in Spanish. There was a rippling of action on board as the tiller man swung the little boat around.

As they came closer Ed could see lots of dirty jeans and fake Hawaiian shirts. They looked like a horrifying parody of a men's fishing trip. The single rod they used to affect this charade was a dead giveaway. It was the type of thing you'd use to battle thousand pound marlin out in the Gulf Stream. If you had any bait. And the rod had a hook and a line. This rod had neither. Ed had worked enough charters to know this outfit was horseshit.

A man to starboard lifted a short, ugly gun from the deck. Ed had never even seen a gun before tonight (not many guns in Bloomfield Hills) and now for the second time in an hour he'd had one stuck in his face.

There were at least four of them. The one in the bow shined the light on him while a guy on the starboard gunwale pointed the gun at his chest and asked menacing questions.

"Quien eres tu?"

Ed stared directly at the man who asked the question, his arms out in front of him, his hands extended in a show of compliance. Spanish. Well, he'd sure enough signed up for Spanish his first year at Chapel Hill, but never really learned much from the class. He'd had trouble conjugating the verbs. Plus he could never remember in which building the class was held.

Ed stared into the business end of several high powered weapons. "Hey fellas, just doing some fishing. I don't understand Spanish, but I don't want trouble here."

Then the tiller man said something, and the man on the gunwale with the gun looked back and then nodded.

Sotto voce he asked, "Amigo, you see the Federales around here?"

"No. Oh, you mean cops?"

"Si."

"Yeah, they were helping me stretch. You just missed them."

He had their interest. Convinced now that he was neither their rival nor a cop, they relaxed somewhat. They waved him closer. Now only ten feet separated their craft in the still, inky darkness of mid-mangrove water.

"They have gone? Which way? How long?"

"Well, they warned me to get the fuck out of here about, what, about an hour ago?"

"And you didn't leave?"

"I'm *fishing*."

"Si." They nodded among themselves, accepting this. "What did you tell them?"

"I told them I was fishing tarpon. They went back down towards Cow Key channel."

"Si, si. Okay, be careful out here amigo, there are dangerous men about." The man said it with a smile, though.

They restarted their motor and eased back up the channel. Ed decided that after two run-ins with armed gangs to call it a night. He was gonna get some sleep. Maybe talk to Stubby in the morning about getting that deposit money so he could hit the road. Three hard strokes to starboard swung the bow around and he started to dig for home.

***

9

Ed was almost home when they caught up to him. The whine of the outboard grew louder behind him. Too late to hide. He reassured himself that if they wanted trouble they'd have fucked him up back in the mangroves. He looked over his shoulder. Their craft looked different. And now it wasn't alone. It was weighed down with…something. Something huge. Barely recognizable now, the fake Whaler was leading a ragged flotilla up the channel.

A round tarp-covered hump, behind which the tiller man had to stand up to see over, weighed the boat to its rails, threatening to swamp it. He watched as the man waved and smiled, then eased the Whaler right up to the kayak, bumping it slightly. They were just a hundred feet beyond the lights at the end of the dock. Hector reached down for something at his feet. Ed thought it would be a gun, but it was too big, the guy was straining to lift it. It looked like a smooth black rock.

He swung it over the rail and it landed with a splash on the kayak, nearly tipping Ed into the water. He was about to protest when the guy swung over another and gave the bale a little pat with his hand.

"For your trouble, amigo. Gracias." The man smiled and nodded. And he wound up the little outboard, pointed the tiller toward Ed and the bow swung off towards the horizon and the little fake Whaler hurried to catch up to the convoy. A gap opened in the clouds, and Ed could just make out the dark shape of a ship, sans lights, bobbing at anchor on the horizon, a few miles offshore. Just beyond a treacherous reef system and at the edge of deeper waters to the south and east. There were maybe five boats, each driven by a member of the crazy fishing party. They were all stacked up. Some of the boats even pulled loaded dinghies. It looked like every available craft that they could beg, borrow or steal on short notice was loaded with contraband. It was a motley crew. They motored uneasily out towards the ship, bobbing and tipping in the currents and small waves. A sloppy operation. Ed noticed a few bales tumble off one of the boats into the water. The guy driving just looked back, hesitated, and kept going.

Ed's leg was getting wet now, his kayak was taking on water. He counterbalanced and paddled that last few feet up to the dock in front of the marina, quiet now in the post midnight gloom. With effort he managed to push the bundles up onto the dock. He eased out, his legs stiff from hours in the cockpit, and climbed the slimy metal ladder up to the dock and stood over the bundles. He looked around. He gave one bundle a little kick. It was solid and heavy, but gave a little where his foot clipped it.

Ed was alone on the dock with the two bundles. A wave of electricity rushed through him. He cast around frantically, sure that he was about to be tackled, or shot, or arrested.

Get those fucking dogs off me!

My leg!

But all was quiet. Gauzy yellow light filtered down from the towers and cast deep shadows around the marina. When he'd triple checked that the coast was clear (and the coast was hardly *clear* as it crackled with eager lawmen and armed smugglers and wild eyed partisans) he moved the bundles into a motorless Mako 19' that sat nearby on blocks. He looked around. Dark and quiet. No one around. The only sound was the distant shout of the drunks down at Hogfish, a few hundred yards on the opposite end of the marina. He went to get his car.

His steps were quick and nervous, he turned up Cyprus Street, trying hard not to hurry, sure that everyone…just *knew*. He walked with his head down, trying not to attract any attention. His heart was slamming away. *Think, goddammit, think. C'mon Ed!*

***

Fifteen hundred miles due north, Danny Stewart set a few more pint glasses in the pale green plastic tray, slammed the door shut and punched the button for Auto Wash-HOT, then took another order. Four Broad Shoulder Ales. Check. He quickly drew the headless drafts and took the next order before collecting money for the first. It was getting busy now, the usual Friday night crush of suits. Just another round and one more expensed drink to fight the boredom and loneliness of another train ride out to suburbs. Danny was setting them up, and they were knocking them down. While the tip jar was relatively empty even for approaching seven o'clock, Danny knew the real cake was when these guys signed for the tab. Bleary eyed and unsure of whether they'd bought four rounds (or was it seven rounds?) for the guys in Finance. It was all expensed anyway, so fuck it! It was busy nudging frantic, stacked three deep at the bar, shiny shoes desperate for traction on slippery tiles as they wedged closer to the bar and the sweet comfort offered there at nine bucks a pour.

Just keep moving forward, throw an elbow if you have to—s'cuse me, fella!—but get another round, because a VP just invited you to join his table and this could be it! I need four fucking Belvedere martinis over here, huh? Bartender!

And the crazier it got, and the louder and hotter it got, and the more drinks spilled and the more people who came in and the more glasses broken, the more Danny relaxed. He was one serene cat in the middle of a Chinese fire drill, affected but in a contrarian way. Things slowed for him, decisions came easy. Just keep pouring. The bar was the barrier. Barbarians at the gate! Keep the drinks moving out and the money coming in.

And in walked one of the biggest fish in the financial district, "Crazy" Joe Steamer, the hedge fund wunderkind and free spender. A guy who avalanched cash wherever he went and always with a smile, always with a sense of reckless free will. A goddamned walking affirmation of the power of the free market to make a wildly aggressive alpha male a millionaire (way) before he turned thirty. If ever there was free money, this was it, and Danny knew it. From Dab's place in Lincoln Park it was only a short ride on the El, it was worth it to come down to the financial district and pour single malts for the Executive Dining Room crowd. It paid well. His savings was filling up now, nearly four grand now, but to what end? He'd graduated Madison and was in Chicago to stay in the extra room of his buddy Dab who ended up trading derivatives and making so much money he didn't know what to do with it. It had been a fun summer, but with Labor Day he started to wonder what he was doing. His tie was choking him a little; giving his round face even more of a red puffy sheen, and sweat lined his brow and ran down his sides, starting to soak his white cotton shirt.

He was taking drink orders from young, rich assholes. And he wondered if he was missing something.

Bartender. *Bartender! Five more of...these!*

***

That night at the Cat Club on Lexington, Houston, Texas, U.S. of A., Harlan "Nut" Richards was ordering another round for his party. The rounds—of which they were nine or twelve deep—were running about eighty-five dollars per and they were still on the shy side of nine o'clock. At the table were Strock Bishop and J. Sloan Pickett. Like him, oil men. But unlike him, they had ranches. That seemed the next logical step. Heck, they were ten years older than him anyway. But still...it bugged him. Now, old Nut, he wasn't doing too bad: a titular oil company, an eight thousand square foot house in Clear Lake, two helicopters, a seventy-two foot sportfisherman docked in Galveston, vast holdings in the Permian basin, hundreds of derricks, always running, pumping, pumping, pumping....

But it wasn't enough. Something was missing for Nut. Something, a void perhaps, that he'd felt since his days running the sweep at SMU had ended. He wanted to do something major, something to set him apart from the mere millionaires, of which there were many in Houston. Too many. He needed to get out there, make his mark, if he could only—

"Say Nut, look at the udders on *that* one!" called Bishop. Nut turned to check out the dancer. Tiffani Crystal was shaking her enhanced mammary glands to the delight of the assembled stockbrokers, oil magnates and real estate land rape specialists. The Cat Club did pretty well, and with whopping cover charges and twelve-dollar bottles of Budweiser, they were able to keep the hoi polloi at bay.

The three men exchanged ideas in the slang vernacular and talked about business. After about fifteen minutes of listening to Pickett's tales of three ways with Filipina hookers and Bishop's hyperbolic tales of conquest, fueled, as they were, more by Gelnnfiddich than reality, Nut had heard enough. Hell, if he wanted to hear people talk like drunken dockworkers, he could visit his rigs outside Odessa. No, tonight was different. Tonight he wanted to know about ranches. He had his mind on getting out of the old boom/bust oil business permanently. And he wanted to get these two titans' opinions on the best place to buy some ranch land.

So carefully he broached the subject, and soon they were filling his head with tales of life on the range. And of course, if you got bored out there, you could just send a helicopter to Dallas and get some gash sent out via airmail.

***

Danny was running the checks now. Tired and still sweating, but this was the fun part. Settling up. He enjoyed his first cold beer of the night. The dirty beer, before he'd had a chance to even wash his face. He stood at the corner of the bar while the manager cashed them out for the shift. He scanned his pile of receipts and punched the numbers into a cheap calculator…seven bucks…twenty-three….thirty….twenty… fifteen…one!...(cheap fucker! he remembered the guy, too, a piker in a fake Armani)…twenty…fifteen…

***

Nut was having a good time. The booze had him feeling just about right. It had been a long day.

13

He wanted to get set up, get a ranch, and start living The Life. Something these two knew about. Hell, Rogers hadn't lifted a finger since he sold his first drilling contract in '62. Bishop was the kind of guy born on third base who thought he'd hit a triple. Still, they had the money. But it wasn't what Richards wanted, he wanted that cache that only owning a ranch could bring. That's where these two guys came in. He wanted to ask them about getting a ranch. Getting set up.

"Well, Nut, this sure has been good time," said Rogers, a tall and voluble man in a string tie. His clipped white hair gave him a stately bearing. "But as you know, I've got a wife to get home to."

"And a mistress to visit on the way," said Bishop, and they all fell out laughing.

***

Danny sat by the window of the Brown Line and watched the neighborhoods blur, the wash of lights soothing, the muted click-clack of the steel wheels underneath spread out past neighborhoods—next stop Armitage—next stop Diversey—carried him home again. It had been a good night, almost two bills, but he was careful not to grab the knot in his right pocket. Don't draw any attention to yourself, especially not this close to Cabrini Green. Just get home and pack a bowl and let Jerry and the boys sing you to sleep.

Tonight, tending bar.

Next stop, oblivion.

Click-clack, click-clack.

It was after twelve when he got off the El and started to walk up Sheffield Avenue towards his apartment. Well, Dab's apartment. Dab was Michael Adam Horowitz III, Danny's best friend and the most ambitious person he'd ever met.

He was Danny's roommate from his first semester at Witte house. Danny was a freshman then, the starting center-half on the soccer team. And Dab was just beginning to dabble in the many business ventures, dabble in stock trading and dabble in a lot of things that eventually earned him his nickname. He'd been referred to as Trey in high school, since he was Horowitz the Third, but Dab had stuck since that first semester in Madison. They were still tight. Even though Danny was an overeducated bartender and Dab made eight hundred and forty thousand dollars last year, their respect was deep and mutual. They had been idiot freshmen together. Many times they'd pooled their dough to buy a seven-dollar pizza.

After a brief walk Danny was buzzed into the marble foyer by the doorman, and ascended the gilded elevator to Dab's co-op. Three thousand square feet with a pool table and a library, not bad for your first crib, barely a year out of college. Of course, trading commodity futures for Brist & Hadley was hardly a typical entry-level job. Dab had let Danny stay in a side room rent free for the summer, just to have someone to hang with. Most of the other traders, and certainly all of the finance guys, were from the University of Chicago and Harvard and the Wharton School and Dab always got the feeling that they looked down on a plebian Wisconsin-Madison graduate. They were nice enough guys, well mannered, and they had to respect his preternatural ability to make money for the firm, for he was the top dog in a room full of aggressively successful money riskers, but he never really hit it off with them socially. Anyway, he felt better hanging with a fellow Badger.

"How'd it go, champ?" he asked as Danny walked in.

"Good night, you know? About two bills."

"Swank. Well, I was just about to load up the dingo if you're interested."

"Giggin."

And they packed a bowl and Dab punched a button on the remote. Soon Peter Tosh was easy skanking from speakers the size of a Toyota. The sweet smell of high grade marijuana filled the air. The bass was thumping. It shook the room. And the two old friends sat deep in the massive leather couch, kicked their feet up and shared a bowl. They drifted and talked of the upcoming Labor Day Weekend parties. Should they go up to Dab's parent's place at the lake? Or maybe Dembowski's cookout?

Their talk grew animated; outside the open windows, summertime rolled. Different music, a piss break. Now they were drinking Bushmills from icy tumblers up on the roof deck. They were laughing about the old days, just a few years ago, running around Witte in the student ghetto at Madison, trying to get laid, but usually just getting drunk. And they laughed and smiled and their heads flowed wide open, and they looked out over the bright lights of the big city of Chicago.

Chapter Two

Ed pulled into the Burger King on the right, halfway to Miami now, and checked his watch. Just minutes to spare. It had been a high speed early morning wobble, the old beater coughing smoke all the way up US-1. He didn't want to drive so fast, but if he missed this call he was fucked. The stuff was in the trunk, covered with whatever sheets and tarps he could round up on (extremely) short notice. It was all happening. Surreal. In a flurry of pre-dawn phone calls he'd finally gotten word to Sponge through an intermediary. Now he was waiting for a call at a payphone on the brick wall in back by the drive through sign.

Even expecting the call, Ed jumped when the phone rang. Right on time. A brief, cryptic conversation ensued. No names were used. With extreme reluctance Sponge had given him an address in Miami. No name, no phone number. Danny was to present himself there and state his case. After that, he was on his own. Under no circumstances was he to mention's Sponge's name.

"You understand that, motherfucker? No names. This gets back to me and you'll be searching for your scrotum through a telescope."

"I understand, man. Thanks."

So with a Miami address scribbled on a napkin, and with enough chafless Kali Mist buds in the trunk to put him away—not for possession, either, but for trafficking—Ed put on his right blinker and eased out of the greasy parking lot and onto the northbound gray cement of US-1. He thought about money and second chances and jail while he cruised past brightly painted bungalows and endless billboards advertising cheap seafood specials and t-shirts and discount dive charters.

***

Danny rolled out of bed sometime after eleven. He had just enough of a hangover to remind him that he'd had a good time the night before. He loaded some munitions into the dingo, blazed, then grabbed a big glass of orange juice from the fridge.

Another endless day stretched before him. He'd have to be back at the bar by eight, but that was a long ways off. Thoughts drifting, pleasant wonder. He flipped through Dab's magazines—Forbes, Barron's—and felt incredulous. He read about guys launching start-ups, billion dollar deals, millionaires by thirty. One success story after another. The principles always talked about hard work, value added. Danny wondered how much hard work was really required to make a half million dollars on one deal. Some work, sure, and some specialized knowledge, like an MBA or something, but come on! Somewhere in there the line between hard work and gluttonous greed got real blurry.

And he thought about when he broke two bills in one shift, and how that felt like good money. He thought that wouldn't buy these dudes a pair of shoes, probably. On page 117 of Worth he saw a little sidebar about "Crazy" Jim Steamer and how he'd just lead a four hundred million dollar initial public offering. Danny wondered where it all ended. Hell, if he had a fraction of that money he'd just retire now. Maybe get a camper van. What was the point of making more money that you could ever spend? Imagine doing that for a living! Every day.

Then again, what was the point of getting idiots drunk every night?

Danny wondered where he fit in to it all. The son of a drywall installer, his mother a part time waitress. He'd been the first in his family to go to college and now he spent his time carefully pouring beer into tall glasses only so assholes could spill it on the floor.

He put the magazine down because it was depressing him. He sure as hell didn't want to pour drinks his whole life, but he didn't know what else he wanted. He couldn't do Dab's kind of work, which he considered a rip off. An investment bank is a tool for wealth extraction was the way Dab had described it to him. So that was out. And law school was out, no way he was joining that unhappy fraternity. Danny wasn't sure what that left him. He liked hiking and camping. Tough to make a living at that. To really *do*…something. He was reloading the dingo when he noticed a brightly colored DVD lying by the stereo. Looked cool. So he threw it on.

The film began. And immediately—something—clicked. He couldn't look away. Something moved deep inside him.

***

Ed shook the old milk jug, trying to guess how much it held. A season's worth of loose quarters and nickels, it now represented his net worth. The fuel gauge read almost empty, it was gonna be a close call. The deal had him worried. Thanks to Sponge he knew what he had and roughly how much it was worth to men at various levels of the distribution network. But he had no idea what kind of coked up cowboys he was gonna be dealing with in Miami. Was he walking into an ambush? A shakedown? Cops? He kept trying to tell himself –

FUCK!

It was already too late.

The cop had been hiding behind a billboard at the end of the bridge onto Islamorada. A hulking figure in black leather. As Ed flew past, the Highway Patrolman stowed his radar gun and came roaring out into traffic, his bike wound up to a roar. His worst fears realized, Ed watched this Shock Horror unfold in his rearview mirror.

So, they had been waiting for him all along!

The cop was flying. His lights flashed. Cars were scattering in front of him. He was closing fast. Ed rehearsed his alibi and got ready to pull over.

***

Nut was at the helm. His thick right hand rested on the steering wheel as he guided the Viking 72' out of Galveston Bay. Barefoot with shorts on, he was as relaxed as he got. Hell, it was Labor Day Weekend! And he'd invited a few guests to join him. On board were ten cases of beer, twelve bottles of Cristal and five party girls. Their ages averaged about sixty percent of his forty one years. How they cooed and laughed at his wit, eager to get his next drink. He was used to it. Hell, he'd never had to look far. He'd learned early. When you play football in Texas, even in junior high, you can pull all the wool you want. And for an oil tycoon with his own helicopter, heck, it wuddn't that hard either.

He thought about what the boys had told him the night before, a man with no ranch is a like tits on a bull. Useless. He knew they were right. Drilling was passé. Too seventies! The real future, they had told him, was in derivatives trading. Hell, look at Enron, right down the street. Geeks—geeks!—over there making a million-a-year trading…what? Trading not oil, not assets, but contracts. Derivates. Futures and options, puts and calls. Bishop and Pickett had tried explaining it to him, but by then his brain was floating on a sea of single malt.

Only thing made sense was oil. Oil he knew. But at twelve dollars a barrel on the world spot market, he could see it was time to bail. Get out while the getting's good. He thought about all the alternatives his advisors had run by him, and they all melted into a blur. One thing that stood out was the ski area. A few years back he'd gone up to Steamboat with a buddy of his, Scooter Williams, a full back who cleared holes for Nut when the two of them were running the sweep at SMU. And it had been great. He barely skied, but his fun was enhanced when he fucked a few waitresses before the week was out. Yep, he could see himself up there in *Coloradah* sipping single malts and getting his knob polished.

***

Ed's mouth was dry. Thunder exploded behind his ears. His eyes were glued to the Highway Patrol cop currently speeding up behind him. Here he was, wide open and exposed on the most saturated smuggling road in America. Guilty as fuck. Nowhere to run, no side roads, just a sinewy line of pavement sweeping him northeast towards America, interspersed with tropical atolls and t-shirt shops. With an old junker belching smoke, himself a sweaty mess, a jangle of nerves in desperate need of sleep or a shower, he felt raw. Why hadn't he just kicked these goddamn bundles into the water? Now he was gonna spend the rest of his life in jail.

He was gonna stick to his story no matter what. The trunk hadn't opened since he bought this old beater, and he was on his way to Agnes Scott college in Atlanta to visit his girlfriend. It might work for the unambitious, end of shift types just trying to hit their daily ticket quota. But this cop bore none of that shiftlessness on his sleeve. He looked more like the Angel of Death roaring up from Satan's Cage. Death blood, fire, kicking heads in, his shiny black boots a vicious mess of skull and brain while he laughed. Blood and death in the mid day sun.

Yep, this is patrolman Jenkins, we're not gonna need that ambulance, Over. Yep, just send the hearse.

Ed wondered if he could just pull over and make a run for the ocean. Obviously, they'd launch patrol boats and helicopters and shoot him like a dog, his blood leaking out into the sea from his bullet riddled corpse…but it would buy him some time. He'd just about convinced himself that he would bolt from the car on first opportunity—or maybe just back over the guy's bike when he approached the car, then peel out and duck the inevitable hale of bullets that would explode toward the back of his head. Fear. Trembling. Adrenaline.

Just then the car behind Ed started to pull over and the last remaining obstacle between him and Death Cop was removed. This was it. It had taken about thirty seconds. And just as Ed eased off the gas and was about to flip his turn indicator to the right, the cop slowed down, following the trailing car to the shoulder. The *other* guy got pulled over!

He kept doing the speed limit and sweating, wondering how long his luck would hold out. The miles crawled by.

Sometime later Nut woke up and rubbed his face. He leaned over the bare ass of the girl next to him and grabbed his phone. He punched a key with his thick fingers and soon Degbert was on the line.

"Degs, you know that ski area we talked about? Buy it. Yeah, sign my name to a tender offer at nine. Make it happen." And he hung up, and the girl nuzzled close to him.

"Did you get some sleep, honey pie?"

"Go get me an OJ, honey."

***

The last of the milk bottle had bought Ed half a tank of gas and a small paper cup full of disgusting coffee. Ed knew little of Miami. Leery of asking directions with such a delicate cargo in his trunk, he opted to drive around to orient himself. He'd burned some precious gas—and driven through some neighborhoods that looked like tropical demilitarized zones—but soon found himself in Coral Gables. The houses were Mediterranean manses, bright as alabaster in the morning sun, with red clay tile roofing. The lawns were impossibly green. His old jalopy stood out in a neighborhood full of status toys. He pulled up in front of 1150 Sundown.

Nervous about pulling his old junker into the half circular driveway with a Hummer and a Porsche, he pulled down a couple of blocks and parked on the street. Ridiculously, he locked the car. He walked towards the big house.

He'd imagined a roomful of sweaty, nervous Cubans. Darkened corners where armed thugs stood ready to stomp his brains in. Rip offs. Guns. Worse.

He was ready for anything. But this? The neighborhood, the whole area, was in a state of mid-morning idyll. Hardly a palm frond or flowerbed was out of place in any direction. The desperate eyes of the smugglers seemed a million years ago. What if it was a set up? How would he know the guy was on the level? Could he recognize an undercover cop?

He figured he'd slow play the situation. Not mention anything until the guy had already committed something. Fuck, I don't know! What if they just shoot me?

Easy Ed gathered himself and lifted the brass pineapple knocker. Almost immediately the door opened. A buff and tan fella not much older than Ed stood there, smiling faintly, his eyebrows raised. The kind of guy who looked perpetually relaxed, his long sandy blond hair swept behind his ears and down his bare shoulders. He wore only board shorts. Ed quickly realized he must look like shit in his sweaty clothes.

"What's up?" Neutral. Genuine?

"Hi, I'm…Ed." Big mistake! Never use your real name!

"What's up, Ed?"

"I have ahh…can I come in?" he looked nervously to the street behind him.

"Who are you looking for?"

Fuck, fuck! Think!

"Well, I…can't rightly say. That is, I'm not sure whom I'm supposed to talk to, but I might have something here, for someone, who may be interested in making a purchase. Or a perusal, at least, of some… samples…I have for sale. In my car."

"You selling Amway, bro?"

"Nothing like that. More of an agricultural product, I guess you could say. In my car."

The guy scanned the street in both directions. "Lemme guess… *that's* your car?"

"Fraid so."

The guy said nothing.

"OK man, I don't really know how this works, but I have something in my car and a…friend"—Scrotum through a telescope! Some friend! (With friends like these…)—"a friend of mine told me I might be able to stop by here and talk to someone about a sale. Is there someone here in charge of that end of it?"

"There may be some interest. Depends on what you have. I hope we're not talking about like vintage Star Wars figures here."

"This would be more like the Death Star."

There was a pause.

Then the guy scowled. And the tropical air felt very hot on Ed now. "Ok, I might be interested. Now, look at me closely…are you a police officer or a member of the Dade County drug task force? Are you or have you ever been an agent of the local, state or federal law enforcement? Or DEA?"

"Naw, man. My name's Ed. I'm a fly fishing guide and I'm scared shitless."

The guy looked at him for a long moment. Then he smiled. "Why don't you come in? I'm Tony. You wanna take a piss or anything, get washed up a bit before we talk? No offence bro, but you look like you got shot at and missed and shit at and hit."

"Yeah, man, that sounds great."

"Bathroom's down here."

Ed went down the hallway, under the wrap-around staircase leading to the second floor landing, and found the bathroom. It was a verdant hanging garden with a two-story waterfall in one corner. After he'd taken a piss and washed his face, he ran the soft towel across his face and felt slightly better. This guy seemed all right. Right?

He found Tony out back by the pool, talking on the phone while being rubbed with coconut oil by a girl who was wearing most of a bathing suit. Player, thought Ed.

"Tony had to take this call," said the knockout from behind him on the patio. He turned. "It's from Atlanta," she added importantly.

"Oh, I see." Said Ed. He didn't see shit.

"Make yourself at home while he finishes up. Can I get you a pina colada?"

"That does sound good, but I'm gonna just go check on the car."

"All right Eddie, I'll have it waiting when you get back," she called after him.

Ed cut across the lawn just in time to see the tow truck hooking the front of his car.

"Hey, wait!" Sprinting, he tried to cover the two blocks before this sleeveless mutt drove away with his last chance.

"*Waaaaaiiiittt!*"

***

As you drive west out of Denver on raging I-70, up the foothills of the Front Range and through the Eisenhower Tunnel and into the Rockies you'll see wild bighorn sheep skittering around the impossibly steep slopes that occasionally bracket the highway and make the tops of the soaring pine trees invisible unless you pull over and get out and look directly up. Interstate 70 is a humming live wire plugged directly into snow country and as you drive you pass some of the best ski terrain on earth.

You can't go too far wrong. If you go straight on 70 you'll pass sprawling Vail, the largest ski area in the state. Slide over Hoosier Pass you'll find the 24-hour-party people of Breckenridge. Down Colorado Highway 82 you'll find Aspen, where the skiing is so good that the billionaires are pushing out the millionaires. Drive to Route 45 and take a left. You'll be in Telluride; a quaint hamlet in a stately box canyon.

At Arapahoe Basin (that's A-Basin to the locals) you'll find long hairs camped out in the parking lot. Down in Crested Butte you'll find some of the sickest steeps Colorado has to offer. And out to the northwest on Route 40 you'll find the deep snow, sunshine and perfectly spaced trees of Steamboat.

And if you get totally fucking lost you might accidentally run out of gas in Winterland.

Chapter Three

The deal was simple. Nut would submit a tender offer of nine hundred thousand dollars, backed by newly issued company debentures; the boys at Goldman Sachs were handling that scrap in hopes of future feasts. It would take less than a month to go through. That was for the mountain, the lodge and the business. Plus forty acres of under-developed plots. Then they'd set about upgrading the underfunded ski area itself—probably another five million there—starting with massive real estate development. Mixed use, pedestrian village, time shares, shops, the whole muggilacutty. Of course, contractors and sub-men would fight it out to do the actual building. Richards Oil would bear none of the risk. They were just the lead dog on this deal.

But with each division and sub-division, each land deal, with each bid and with each contract, they'd take a toll. With the name Richards Oil writ large on the project it would act like a beacon to developers; a gold seal deal. For a toll. A haircut, as Nut liked to say. And that haircut would line the coffers for years to come. It offered the kind of predictable quarterly earnings that bankers loved and Wall Street rewarded. And it was gonna be the first step in a deal that successfully diversified Nut while making Degbert, his financial whiz kid, look like a hero.

Degbert, thin and blond, wore small steel rimmed glasses. Red suspenders hung over his white work shirt. He hurtled from Houston at eight hundred miles an hour, the Richards Oil jet gleaming in the sun. He punched numbers into his BA-II calculator. He wondered what manner of man he'd be dealing with on this thing. You never knew in Colorado, not any more. You might be grappling with some thrifty cowpokes, fourth generation ranchers who knew the value of their dirt. Or it could be some protean Texan speculator, or lately, a southern Californian developer. Each with money to burn and an eye for big land. Maybe even a Japanese investor…you could be dealing with anyone up there. But Degbert knew he could outsmart them if he wanted to and outbid them if he had to. Gulf Coast Oil had tried to block Nut's takeover bid in '91. Degbert made a name for himself when he ensured that for their defiance Gulf Coast's CEO and most of their board got scorched in a very public way. If he could run over a third generation Texas oil concern roughshod, he could deal with Winterland. Hell, these rubes didn't even have the business acumen to build a real base lodge.

Degbert was flying up there on a due diligence trip. Then he could take this to Nut, after it was teed up. Degbert knew that in the right hands it could be a little gold mine. Other ski areas were making a killing. During their meeting the guys at Goldman who'd handled the private bond placement had informed him that, among other things, a family on a ski trip in Colorado spent an average of a thousand dollars a day.

But see, Winterland was no ordinary ski town. First opened in 1947 by a group of former Tenth Mountain Division soldiers on land purchased cheap from the National Forrest, it had a checkered past. A history of bitter disappointments followed just as many hopeful starts. Through a series of owners it had been through bankruptcy court (twice), then sold at auction, then resold many times over. Usually at a loss.

The ski area had problems. It was small. Its vertical drop was a paltry twelve hundred feet (Steamboat and Vail were each over 3500). It was hard to get to. Isolated in the northwest quadrant of the state it was closer to the badlands of Wyoming than to the population centers of Denver and the Front Range. Far from the nearest interstate, it was a forgotten outpost. Its eastern flank was protected by treacherous Fox Tail Pass. Intimidating in *summer* by wintertime Fox Tail was a downhill ribbon of ice. To the west, the hills melted into barren plains stretching towards Salt Lake City, eight hours drive if you were flying. Winterland was out there. Isolated and barren, it was almost uniquely unsuited to attract well-heeled skiers. There were no amenities, there were no slope side condos and there was no sushi.

And if Winterland Ski Area was struggling, the town with which it shared a name was a basket case. When, after eighty years in business, The Double ZZ Cattle Company was suddenly sold to a real estate investment trust out of Dallas, new jobs had been promised by the bushel. But when the holding company went belly up in the '87 crash (more a victim of wild-eyed land speculation and layers of disastrous financial deregulation under Reaganomics than the incompetent new owners on which its collapsed was locally blamed) the town was devastated. The cattle yard—for whom one in four in the town had worked—laid people off en masse. The boxcars that used to haul valley beef to markets as distant as Chicago and Seattle sat rusting on the tracks. The sheriff deserted the second time his paycheck bounced. The tax base crumbled and many residents fled in search of work. Fewer than a thousand hearty souls remained. Weeds grew through cracked sidewalks. Shops closed. Main Street a checkerboard of white washed windows. The ones who remained were left with mortgage payments to make, kids to feed and a twice-shy reluctance to ever again listen to big promises from outsiders.

Through it all, echoes of the cowboy tradition held strong. In Winterland the rodeo ground was four times the size of the high school football stadium. In popularity, the ski area ranked an almost irrelevant third.

Still, the hill had its share of devotees. Priced out of Vail and Beaver Creek (and all but *chased* out of Aspen) and attracted by the bargain basement rents, a growing number of artists and ski bums had started to arrive. Word was out. And among the nomadic hordes who spent their summer on tour with Widespread selling goo balls in the parking lot, or guiding white water trips, or banging nails all summer to buy a ski pass, they heard about this place called Winterland. Where a season pass was $299, brah. So they lit out. In beat Subarus and rusty microbuses, they braved the Pass and, imperceptibly at first, started to change the character of the town. And what you had there was a mini renaissance in an unlikely place that looked like it just might become a ghost town and pass into the collective memory of the West.

But the new scene was funky fresh. Increasingly you had hackey-sackers in front of the Wells Fargo. Girls with dreadlocks painted portraits on Main Street for ten bucks. And they all seemed to have dogs. In summer the arrivistes played bongos on the town square every evening at sunset. Seemed like every year there were more of 'em. Tie dyed and glassy eyed—they kept on coming. Most folks in the town looked on with bemused disbelief, for the least welcome guy in the West was always the last one over the pass. But for the locals with empty rooms and failing diners the freaks were as welcome as rain in a drought, because even if their hair was green, so was their money.

Chapter Four

Ed almost caught the guy, screaming the whole time for him to stop, he covered the two blocks at a sprint. The tow driver initially pretended not to hear, but when Ed got close enough to bang on the side of the truck, the guy just laughed and shook his head.

Then the stupid hick pulled away with the car, and the dope and Ed's whole fucking life. Even the milk bucket! He was left on the street in a cloud of diesel exhaust.

***

Degbert and Nut sat in the big conference room. The offer was in play, it had gone out first thing that morning. Nine hundred large. And they could go many times over that and still make a pile. Degbert ticked off the list of things they could do, financial maneuvers to cover the deal six ways to Sunday.

"What if I get outbid? What if we can't sell any of the land?"

"Nut, don't worry. We don't have to sell shit. That's for the developer to worry about. We just own the ski area and a few parcels of adjoining land. The developer takes some of the profit, but all of the risk. We don't sell him the land, we offer them a favorable lease." It went without saying to whom the lease would be favorable. "He can get rich or he can go belly up. We get paid either way."

"How's that?"

"We bring a lot to the table, but it's mostly intangibles, very little of it is capital investment. When word gets out that mighty Richards Oil is buying a ski area, they'll be champing to get a piece of the action. Remember when we did the deal in Midland? How much did we stake?"

"'Bout three hundred grand."

"Two seventy nine and change. And what was our profit on that deal?"

"You tell me."

"Four point three million when we sold it, plus the dividends."

"Oh, them haircuts."

"Right. Lots of little haircuts. We're *still* getting paid on that one."

"And this deal will be like that?"

"It will be better. See, we're gonna rebuild this ski area. Modernize the lifts, better snowmaking; get some people up there for once. That's the beauty of this deal. Even while condos are being built, shops and restaurants and a pedestrian village are going up, we're getting monthly preferred dividend deferments from the developers, then when they actually open for business, we get a cut of that, too, since they're doing business on land we own. The mountain itself is the hidden value, and that thing is gonna be a cash cow by the time I'm done with it. We have the potential here for returns on equity approaching forty-eight percent. It's skiing, so we're talking about price inelasticity of demand here. A leptokurtic distribution return."

"Speak English."

"They're gonna get strummed."

"Good stuff, boy. Now, how long 'til bid is accepted?"

"It went out this morning. From what I've been able to uncover the guy who owns the place is in debt up to his ears. He'll jump at the chance to sell."

***

Danny quit his job that night. Told his boss he had to get on the road, but thanks for everything, Brad. The film had lit in him a fire. He'd watched it three times now, and every time he did, the flames roared higher. Ball the jack and just fucking go, man. The West is the Best.

***

Close to panic, Ed rushed back to the house, where he found the door had been locked. A rip off! He knew it. He started to pound with both fists.

"Open this God Damned door!"

One of the blond hotties opened the door, startled at this crude interruption.

"Eddie, what's wrong?" He ignored her, sprinted through the house and found Tony out back. He was asleep.

"Dude!"

"Yehp?" said Tony, not bothering to open his eyes.

"My fucking car just got towed. Now I've got nothing! We have to find that tow truck before they figure out what's in the trunk."

"Easy, bro."

"Easy? I'm fucked, here! You're fucked, we have nothing, we have no deal, here."

Tony's insouciance was really pissing him off. He wanted to kick the guy.

"I know who towed your car."

"You do?"

"In fact, I called them myself."

"*You* called them? Why the fuck did you call them?"

"Let me tell you a story, Ed."

***

Inside the dark ski patrol shack/snowmobile garage/corporate headquarters of Winterland Ski Area the fax machine whirred to life. A document curled out of the creaking Brother—a relic from 1991, now sporting coffee stains, Rosignol ski stickers with a bent coat hanger for the paper feed—and spilled to the floor. It contained a complex bid from something called the Galveston & Colorado Ski Partners LLC. It was Nut's offer. The fifteenth and final page curled to the floor. And then the fax machine went back to sleep. The explosive fax, the one that would forever change the history of Winterland Ski Area, had arrived.

It would go unnoticed for over a month.

***

During a frantic daylong effort that carried him all over North Side, Danny had sold his collection of vintage vinyl, emptied his savings account, tried (unsuccessfully) to get his gym membership refunded, and gotten his mail forwarded to general delivery, Teton Village, Wyoming. He was moving to Jackson Hole. He'd wait for Dab to get home so he could tell him the plan. And then hit the road. His excitement edged giddy euphoria. This was it.

Hit loaded the dingo and hit PLAY on the stereo.

Part Two
Out With the Truckers
and the Gypsies
and the Billboard Highways

Chapter Five

Dab was surprised to see Danny walk out of the bedroom in shorts and a sweatshirt around seven, when normally he'd be getting into uniform for the bar shift.

"Did that pesky dingo make you late again?" teased Dab.

"Don't you slander the dingo. No, listen man, I gotta go."

"Go where?"

The film had been Danny's before and after moment. He tried to explain to Dab what it had done to him. How it had set in him a fire.

"Lately I've been feeling just, I don't know, that something is wrong, like I'm wasting my time, stumbling through life. Its been great living here, thanks so much, but…tending bar…living in the city… is just…I don't know, pointless. But that film was…there's something happening out there."

They were both quiet for a few moments. Then Dab said "that's awesome man. If that's what you've got to do, then do it."

"Yeah, I see the path now. For the first time."

"Righteous. Now, how about a final dingo session for good luck?"

"Giggin."

They ripped two bowls. Then Dab took Danny out for a fat steak. Back at the apartment, they had a few drinks on the roof deck and Danny was just too excited to sleep. He had planned to leave at first light, but couldn't even wait that long. He was going. Dab offered an Exxon card to cover the gas for the trip to Jackson, but Danny declined. He was flush. He had almost four thousand dollars in his camera bag. He did accept a case of wine and some leftover pizza for road food, then took the elevator down to his car. As he pulled down to the end of block and got ready to turn left onto the wide boulevard, the light turned green. He kept his momentum and wound out to the left in an accelerating g-force turn. Streetlights rushed by his windows. He let out a whoop as he sped down the street and through the sleeping city.

The perfectly timed green light would be the last thing that went well on the trip.

***

35

Ed was somewhere in Tennessee, driving north into a gathering thunderstorm when he grew weary and pulled off the interstate and into the nearest generic motel. He checked in, took a shower and was soon bored by the nine cable channels. He tried to remember phone numbers from years ago. He hadn't talked to these people in years. He finally remembered one and dialed, glancing at the extortionate rates posted next to the phone for long distance calls.

"Hello."

"Jim?"

"Yeah, who's this?"

"Jim, its Ed. Ed Stallings. How are you doing?"

"Easy Ed! How the hell are ya?"

The old friends talked for an hour. About high school, and who was doing what (and who was doing whom).

"So what are you up to now Ed? I guess I haven't seen you since graduation."

"Well, I went to Carolina to play ball, you knew that. But that didn't really work out. Lately I've been living in Key West. Stock Island, actually, which is just over the bridge."

"Awesome man, how's life in Key West?"

"I'm actually out of there now. I'm moving to…ahh. That's kind of why I'm calling. I…I was down in the Keys one night, fishing. Friday before Labor Day."

And it came pouring out. As he spoke he realized how great it felt to verbalize his jangled thoughts.

Ed started with the piss test and proceeded from there. How he'd gotten the guy's address from Sponge, how Tony had called the tow truck. It was a long story, but he just kept going.

"So it turns out this guy—this guy Tony—owns the tow truck that took my car away. Apparently, that's kind of his thing. He moves stuff all over south Florida, all over the south actually, and one of his tricks is he moves the stuff around in the trunks of cars, you need mostly late model American sedans for this apparently, which have the biggest trunks, and the cars all have bum registrations, but that doesn't matter, because the tow truck is owned nice and legal. The drivers are all clean. The stuff's in the car. So even if a cop does pull over the tow guy, which apparently rarely happens anyway, he's got plausible deniability. He doesn't know who the fuck's car this is, why would he know? He just got a call to tow it. This is a legit tow company, right? They really tow cars. They really file taxes. So that's why he had my car towed. And I never even saw it again. It went right into the junk yard and got crushed into a cube. They took the stuff out. His guys went through it, knew straight up that it was chafless Kali Mist and they called Tony, who called a buyer in Atlanta, who apparently handles all the action there, and he made him a cash offer. I never saw the stuff again once I loaded it in the car in front of my trailer on Stock Island. Tony took ten percent finders fee, and the next day—oh, that was the funny thing, even after I calmed down and he explained it all to me, I couldn't get the money right away, and I end up like…I can't go anywhere, right, I have no car now, so this laid back high volume drug dealer that I just met offers to let me stay there, with him, in the mini mansion, with the hot chicks and the pool and everything. So I do. I wanted to keep my eye on the guy anyway, plus I have nothing to do, no money and now no car. I hadn't slept now in two days, so I just crashed. In the morning, there's no money. And we have breakfast! They actually make me breakfast. One of the girls. And Tony comes down at like eleven in this white robe, and we all have breakfast, this ponytail kingpin, two gorgeous model chicks and me in my same clothes that I had been fishing in. And the money never shows up that day either. So we go out for drinks that night. Suddenly I'm going out drinking with these freaks! Like this is normal. He loans me some clothes. And we go all over South Beach, and they know this guy everywhere, we're all cutting lines at nightclubs and its VIP sections with champagne sent over by local heavies. And I'm just *with* these people somehow. And the funny thing is, it's kind of fun. I don't have to pay for anything. Everything is funny to them, all the time. It's a wild scene. A limo takes us home. I pass out. So now it's like afternoon on the second day and a bag shows up. Like a gym bag. A duffle bag. And it's my money. Tony doesn't even count it, just hands it over, tells me it's my cut. And the bag is fucking heavy. So I go upstairs to the room I'd slept in and dump it on the bed. Takes me almost an hour to count it. Just a little less than sixty thousand dollars. Sixty fucking grand! I drove up there with change in the gas tank and now I've got sixty grand in random twenties. Wild, right?"

It was quiet for a moment. Ed felt vulnerable after spilling it all.

"That is wild. Wow. Good for you, I guess. So what now, Ed?"

"I don't know. I need to find a home for this money."

"You know who you should talk to, what about Troy Miller?"

"Oh yeah! Miller. What's his story?"

"Oh, he's doing well. Making a killing, from what I heard. He went out to Denver after college, got a job with Rigity Investments. I think he's head of fixed income for them now. Anyway, yeah, he's doing great. You want his number?"

***

Danny drove through the night. By daybreak he was in Iowa, cruising through Jones County. Soon he'd pick up I-80 and swing west. He still wasn't tired. He was elated. The sun peaked through corn stalks as dawn rolled across the tawny umber of the pasture. Through farms and fields he drove, awash in the solo anonymity of the road. Big American flags painted on barns. He was relaxing in an easy drift, leaning back, just two fingers on the wheel, one hand behind his head, when he was suddenly focused by a terrible sound.

Whump whump whump.

He pulled to the shoulder. Flat right front tire. Crap.

He dug out tools from the back of the ten-year-old Subaru wagon. Soon he was rolling around on the ground next to the car. A guy on a tractor slowly rolled up. He stopped, offered a hand, and Danny waved him off with a smile. The guy kept going, the tractor's huge back wheels in slow motion, a haze of diesel exhaust belching through the popping metal flap atop the exhaust pipe. By the time Danny mounted the donut the farmer was miles up the road that eased through the gently rolling pastureland. Red silos against the sky. Waving maize.

He had a new tire mounted in the next town he came to. Hundred and four bucks. By lunchtime he was again moving west. Images of Jackson Hole drifted before his eyelids. He was twenty minutes down the road when he heard and felt that sickening *whump whump whump.*

A sinking feeling in his stomach, he pulled over and got out. The brand new tire was flat.

***

Ed left a voicemail for Troy Miller. Miller had been captain of the lacrosse team when Ed was a freshman at Cranbrook. Something of a local legend, Miller had reportedly lost his virginity to Miss Haggarty one morning before homeroom. But it was his weekend parties that made him famous. The field behind the paddock at Miller's parent's house was the scene of many a high school keg bash. At three bucks a cup for all the Bud Lite you could swill, he cleaned up. Before he could (legally) drive he was taking in hundreds of dollars every weekend. Miller always knew how to make a fast buck. If there was anyone Ed knew who would

38

know where to invest a few surplus dollars—and not ask (or care) where the money came from—it was Miller.

Ed felt he had to do something with this money, something sort of permanent. This was gonna be his chance. Maybe his last. Eager to distance himself, physically and permanently, from his life in the Keys—and from the raw wound trauma of that drug deal—he just wanted to start fresh.

He'd learned this much: he was temperamentally unsuited to selling drugs. He'd been damaged by that ordeal, it took a physical toll. The wild-eyed desperadoes, the cops, almost busted on Islamorada, the weirdness in Miami…it was too much for him. He longed to establish a life with…well, at least one with less chance of long term incarceration.

Ed was vaguely heading home, north anyway, but dreaded the prospect of meeting with the old man. He thought about paying back all the money he had squandered. Maybe that could make up for things that way. But it was never about money for his dad.

Ed wanted to show that he wasn't just some drunken waste case. That he stood for something. What that thing was, however, was still being formed in his mind.

He could picture the awful scene in the oak paneled study, the old man dubious, himself unable to answer questions about his current life (style). Yeah, it would be a nightmare, one that Ed wished to avoid. He needed to find a home for this money, but he knew the old man was not the place to turn. Not yet, anyway. Any way he sliced it, it was gonna be hard to explain. Part time fly fishing guides don't exactly save up sixty grand in tips.

No, the old man could wait. And with that ordeal mentally postponed, he relaxed. It was a new day. The miles flowed easily. Just him in the blue Pathfinder that he'd bought off a used car lot in Miami now, singing along to the radio with the windows open, the wind from the highway blowing through his hair and the big bag of money tucked under the backseat. For the first time in what seemed like forever, he found himself smiling. Perfect white teeth shone through that smile, along with waves of relief. He never wanted to go through that shit again.

***

"We can't fix it. Rim's damaged. See this?"
Danny didn't see anything.
"Here's your problem."
"Where?"
"There."

39

"I don't believe this. I already bought two brand new tires."

"You could buy fifty tires, this wheel is never gonna take em. It's warped. You need a new rim."

Danny recalled hitting…something…in the morning darkness. "Do you guys sell these rims?"

"Naw. You're gonna hafta call Gilchrest, he can get about anything inside 24 hours. Course, he's closed weekends. Be open Monday."

"He's open on Labor Day, that's great."

"Right, Labor Day. Guess that makes Tuesday."

***

From a payphone in Indiana, Ed finally got through to Miller.

"Great to hear from you Ed, how are you? I've only got about two minutes."

"Doing well man, how about you?"

"So busy I can't see straight, but you know how it is."

"Yeah…sure. So Jimmy said you were rolling out there. Actually, that's kind of why I'm calling. I…(what…saved? stole? found?) have (yeah, *have*) a few bucks that I was thinking about investing, and thought you'd be the guy to talk to."

"OK, well…I don't know what Jimmy told you. But I trade munis…ahh…municipal bonds, for Riggity. So I mean, I know a lot about that market, but in terms of day to day investing, equities or whatever, I mean, you probably know about as much as I do."

"I seriously doubt that," laughed Ed.

"You might be better off calling like a Schwab or a Fidelity, someone like that, open a brokerage account, talk to one of their advisors. I mean, the stuff I'm dealing with is…interest rate swaps and forwards, its all pretty esoteric stuff. Not the thing for mom and pop investors. But shit, there's ten new IPO's every day, you might think about that. MicroGlove.com just opened with a sixty-point pop. Get in on one of those. What kind of money are you looking at, anyway?"

"Oh, about forty grand" said Ed, who wondered why he lied. Talking about the money made it seem more real all the time, but it also made him nervous.

"Well, with something like that, you're probably gonna want to think mutual funds, like for starters, open a Roth IRA, then ask your broker about—actually, wait a minute. I have this…about forty K, huh? This might be…let me run something by you. Hear me out on this."

Chapter Six

Danny lay on the cheap taffeta bedspread in his underwear. The air conditioner made plenty of noise but offered scant cooling. With the shades drawn, the sun still beat through every crack. Dust and particles danced in shafts of light. The air was still and hot. The sun beat mercilessly at the door. Danny lay on his back, sweating in the dark hothouse. He'd taken two showers already, each colder than the last. They offered only temporary relief.

He watched television. He found himself envious of every car chase; at least their cars were moving forward. His car was a disaster. He'd bought it (cheap) during the summer of his junior year in Madison. With money made delivering calzones on campus for seven bucks an hour plus tips. It was a burgundy colored Subaru wagon, and it hadn't given him any trouble until now. He'd been on road trips with that car, up to Dab's place by the lake, camping all over the Upper Peninsula, down to the Kentucky Derby that one time. Yeah, the old Suby had served him well. But the odometer was pushing a deuce and a half.

So he lay there in bed, waiting for Tuesday morning to roll around, when this Gilchrest guy could allegedly get him a new wheel. Danny figured in his head. Gilchrest didn't open 'til Tuesday. Then it would take twenty-four hours to get the part. That made it Wednesday. Even this shit ass motel was still forty-eight bucks a night. When he added that to the two tires already purchased and the cost of the new rim, he was in for close to four (maybe four and a half!) bills right there. Between that, gas and greasy food his grubstake was melting away. And he still needed to buy skis when he got out there. Yikes. He was less than three hundred miles from Chicago. At this rate…

He tried to stop running numbers in his head, it was stressing him out. But it was tough. He had nothing to do but wait. And sweat. And lose money. Until the new wheel came in. (Hopefully) on Wednesday. It was Sunday afternoon.

***

"Well, here's the thing Ed. I bought a business last year. A bar. It's called Trappers, right? It's up in Winterland, that's this little cattle town slash ski area up high in the Rockies. About four and half hours from Denver. Middle of nowhere. Anyway, when I moved out here I got a job with Riggity and had to work the phones for about a year, then I got promoted to trading assistant, then full trader. So a couple of years ago I got my first real bonus. And it was like, a good five figure type bonus. I never saw that kind of money yet, it was pretty exciting. So I'm fully vested here, I have like 401(k), IRA, Roth IRA, we have a profit sharing, so it's like I'm invested up and down the market, so I wanted to diversity a little. I went to a realtor in Boulder that a trader buddy of mine recommended, and told him I had a few dollars to invest, he told me about this bar in Winterland. And I'll be honest with you, this is a matter of public record anyway, but I paid eighty thousand dollars for this place. That's for the business and a long term lease on the property. Put most of it down, and borrowed another thirty to make up the rest. And at first it was great, I went up there some weekends, even tended bar a few times. It was fun. But the bar is struggling. I did the due diligence on the place, saw all the financials for the previous ten years, and they were healthy. Like an annual forty percent return on equity. The mark up on alcohol is like eighty four percent. It all looked kosher. But apparently a couple of years back the big cattle yard closed down and every stiff in town got laid off at once. Now the whole town is teetering on the brink of bankruptcy. Revenue fucking plummeted. So now I'm kind of stuck with this place. And really, it does make some money. Thankfully what people are left in that town sure love to drink, I can show you my returns. But there isn't much upside right now. Stagnant cash flows. What the place needs is a full time, hands on owner. I guess I just wanted to own something cool like a bar, but it's not for me. I don't have time to get the place up to scratch. Anyway, I don't know what your situation is or whatever, but if you wanted to talk about maybe taking over the place, I'm sure I could offer you some pretty favorable terms. You know, seeing as how you helped me stop Mutt Flannigan from stealing my tap at the Halloween Ho Down."

"I'd forgotten about that!" said Ed.

"So anyway, think it over and let me know if you're interested. If so, fly out here and I can show you the paperwork. I don't have the time to run it. I'd be happy just to get rid of it, but it could be something for you. Now I gotta run."

"Cool man, that does sound interesting. Shit yeah. Hey, I'll let you know. When do you need to know by?"

"Oh, no real time frame. Right now the cash registers are enough to cover the note, so I'm not too worried about it. But I'm going short on this bar. I'm getting out. I really gotta hop now."

A bar owner. Ed liked the ring of that. Maybe they had some trout streams out there too, he'd picked up a nice eight-weight at a fly shop north of Miami and was dying to wet a line. Maybe this was just the thing he'd been waiting for. He pulled the Pathfinder into a motel. Bar owner. And so he went to sleep that night with visions of flowing beer taps in his head and when he woke up, he got out his map and started looking for the nearest west bound highway.

***

Eager to escape the heat and boredom of another afternoon in the motel, Danny took a walk. It wasn't so much a town as a glorified truck stop. Gas stations, single story concrete motels with bright yellow signs out front, a few garages, a diner. The highway stretched away in both directions, melting back into the corn. No movie theater or bookstore to pass the time. Everyone in town was old and drove huge American automobiles.

He returned to the dingy motel, wishing he had the dingo to help him pass the time.

Wasted days of inert longing.

The free time didn't ease his mind. He worried. That they wouldn't be able to order the part, or it would be prohibitively expensive, or some other goddamn delay on this trip that he just couldn't seem to get started.

***

On Tuesday morning he was the first one at Gilchrest Motors. Earl Gilchrest Junior pulled in at eight and unlocked the office. He flipped on the stuttering lights and waved Danny in. Gilchrest was short and pudgy and amused.

"Hey, how's it goin?"

"Not bad. I have a flat tire, and they tell me the rim is warped too. Any chance you guys can order one?"

"Yep, we can order it. Just give me a minute till this friggin thing turns over." He slapped the computer on the desk. The monitor's blinking orange fonts revealing its age. "You want a coffee while you wait?"

43

"Sure, sounds great."

"Don't say that til you try it."

Danny poured a coffee, and then dumped the powdered creamer in the styrofoam cup. A massive black and yellow Hawkeye flag covered the back wall. In a few minutes Gilchrest heard a little beep, looked up from his issue of Motor Cycle and called to Danny. "Looks like she's awake. What kind of car is this?"

"Subaru Legacy, eighty-nine. Wagon. It's the front right wheel."

"Eighty…nine…Subaru…wagon? Fifteen by six?"

"Hell, I don't know. You want to take a look, it's parked out front, the one with the donut on it."

"We might be able to help you. You're lucky, we don't usually help foreigners."

Gilchrest pointed to the Badger sticker on Danny's back window.

"Yeah, I played soccer for them."

"Well, least it wasn't football. That's all right, we might help you anyway. Course, I'll have to charge you 'bout double." They both laughed. Just then the first mechanic showed up. Gilchrest spoke to him.

"Pete, go round back and help our misguided little friend here. See if we can't find him a fifteen inch wheel off of something."

They went around to the back of the cinderblock building, in the dirt lot, and stared at tangled piles of debris. Tire pile over here, old mufflers in that pile. Danny watched as Pete cursed and threw chunks of metal around. At length he came out from behind a mound holding a wheel in his hands.

"This'll fit. Just give me about twenty minutes to mount her up and you can be on your way."

"You don't have to order anything?"

"Naw. Lotta times we have extras lying around. Costs more to have em hauled away than to keep em."

"Terrific."

Back in the office Danny found Gilchrest on the phone.

"Wouldn't hear of it, Charlie. That twelve pack was plenty. No, you take care." He hung up. "Pete didn't try to fuck ya, did he?"

"No, he was a very gentle. He actually found me a wheel, he's gonna get my tire mounted on there right now. I'm glad, I didn't want to spend another minute at that motel."

"You scurrying back to cheese land?"

"Other way. Actually, I'm headed out to Jackson Hole, to do some skiing this winter."

"A cheese head on skis." Gilchrest laughed like he'd never heard something so funny.

"What do I owe you for the wheel?"

"Well, with the Wisconsin surcharge, you're looking at twenty large, my friend."

"Twenty bucks?"

"Could be thirty, if ya like."

"No, no, twenty's great. Thanks man."

"You just say 'go Hawkeyes' and you'll be on your way.

"Go Hawkeyes!"

"You have a good time skiing, Badger. Send us a post card."

"Yeah, thank you man." They shook hands. Soon Danny had his car back, the old wheel with the new tire mounted, the bill paid, feeling good. He was ready to get on the road. He gave Gilchrest Motors—about the friendliest bunch of folks he'd ever met—a final wave and pulled back out onto 151. It wasn't even noon. He got on the highway and the town receded in his rearview and he gunned it up to seventy.

Three hours later the clutch let go.

***

"Hello?"

"You have a collect call from a Danny Stewart, will you accept the charges?"

"Sure thing," said Dab.

The operator clicked off.

"Yo."

"What's up champ? How's Jackson Hole?"

"I wish I knew. I'm still in Iowa."

"Iowa? Why?"

"Good question."

***

Dab was on his second beer. It had been a long story.

"Well, now the clutch was busted. I felt it gradually slipping away, it didn't happen like –BANG!- you have no clutch, it just sort of…I could feel it getting closer and closer to the floor, engaging a little later, a little later…and then it was just gone. I was still in Iowa and—I should have known. During pre-season camp we used to run miles for soccer, and we'd sing songs, and one of the favorites was we'd sing—

45

we don't give a damn about the whole state of Iowa,
whole state of Iowa, whole state of Iowa
we don't give a damn about the whole state of Iowa
who the hell likes corn?

I was a captain, I'd be leading the run, so I'd sing the first line, and everyone would shout the second and so forth. Anyway—So it figures I get ramrodded in Iowa. Two tires, now that wheel, which actually was pretty inexpensive, then I had to fix the clutch, and that was after one place wanted fourteen hundred bucks. There was no way I was spending fourteen hundred bucks, the car is worth less than that. So for a while I had to dry shift it."

"Is that like dry humping?"

"You wanna find out?"

"Keep talking, wise guy."

"Anyway, I have to dry shift it. It's a standard, so you basically have to start the car, you know, already in gear, and get her moving. Then time the shifts to the RPM's, without using a clutch. You can do it. It's not difficult, really, but if you miss time any of the shifts you stall. And stalling out on I-80 is not any kind of fun, let me tell ya. So I fucking dry shifted it all the way across Iowa and into Nebraska. Its actually not that bad, once you get up into fifth gear its fine, it's no different than driving any other time. But getting on and off the highway for gas was terrible. But I didn't see the point of getting a brand new clutch on this old ass car. It was so stressful. Finally I'd had enough white knuckling—"

"You were masturbating this whole time, too?"

"You're a funny one. I'd finally had enough…white knuckling [they both laughed] and I had to get it fixed. I just decided to pull over, and for some reason this guy could fix it way cheaper, said it was just the master cylinder, actually, I didn't even need a whole clutch, so it seemed like it was going to go well. It didn't. I end up stuck in another town, Kearney, Nebraska. Which, unfortunately, exists. So they're telling me it's gonna be an easy fix, but they can't get the part. And again I have to waste days and days just sitting there. Every day I go down and check, everyday the part's not in. By this time I'm not even bothering with motels anymore. My money is running low. I left Chicago with almost four bills and I was already getting down to about twenty-two hundred or so, and I'm in fucking Nebraska. Jackson seemed a long way off. I was sleeping in the car. I was parked in the back of this garage that was supposedly ordering me this master cylinder that never showed up. And it was right near the highway, so all I can hear all night long is big rigs jack braking around this bend. I sleep about twenty minutes at a time. Plus there's a vicious German Shepherd in the yard who is philosophically opposed to me getting any sleep. I was stuck there for fucking ever. Days and days. Finally the part comes, it was the wrong part. Everything sucked. I'm living on peanut butter sandwiches and Spaghetti-O's, living in my car like a broken down hobo. I mean, I've been camping, but this is ridiculous. They finally get the right part, and I'm on my way. Five hundred bucks including labor. Oh, and they had tried to hit me with a storage fee for holding the car. I was incredulous. I told them I'd been sleeping in the fucking car, on their property, if anything, acting as free security the whole time. Man, I wanted to punch the guy. Here I am living on fucking c-rations and this hick wants to charge me for the privilege of homelessness. So anyway I'm almost to North Platte now, then I'm gonna duck into Colorado, then swing north to Jackson. I should be there tomorrow."

"Well, shit man, that car is killing you. I'd have freaked. Glad you got it fixed up."

"Yeah, it's been rough. But I'm nearly there. I'm gonna run. This call is probably costing you a fortune."

"Ah, no worries man. Let me know if there's anything I can do to help."

"Thanks man."

"The dingo sends its best."

"Later."

***

Ed drove west on I-70. After the flatiron plains of Kansas—hundreds of miles of wheat colored, endless monotony—he found eastern Colorado to be, disappointingly, just as flat. And just as boring. But within an hour or so the Rockies began to emerge from the horizon, slowly, inexorably. Purple! They lined the horizon in blurry relief, growing slowly, but ever rising, rising, rising from the wheat plains. It was hours before he saw the tall buildings of Denver, by then the hills he had seen that morning, that had looked so huge, were revealed as mere foothills. Precursors to the real action that began behind them, and stretched away back towards another endless horizon. That would be another day. He was tired from the road and pulled into a gas station to call Miller. He figured Miller would still be working, it was only seven o'clock.

Miller gave him directions to a bar on 19th street. An hour later Miller breezed in, carrying a canvas briefcase and about five cell phones and pagers. He immediately ordered fifty dollars worth of drinks and shrimp and oysters. They chatted for a while and caught up. Miller talked about financial chicanery that Ed pretended to understand, and Ed glossed over his past few years while trying to make them sound as productive as possible. Next to Miller's red-blooded embrace of the capitalist ideal, Ed felt like a deadbeat. After several rounds—Miller had made clear early on that he was flipping the check, so order up—they got around to talking about the bar.

"Oh, it's been such a disappointment to me. I thought it would be a great way to diversify. But right now it's stuck in neutral and I'm not about to quit my job to move up there to run it. I really think that all the place needs is a hands on owner to breathe some life into it."

"Well I know my way around a barroom," said Ed.

"Yeah, you and me both. It's dead fucking simple. You have one distributor to deal with, he gets you any beer, wine or liquor you ever heard of. Delivers once a week. You write checks for the distributor and the electricity and you charge money for the drinks. A monkey could do it."

"Mutt Flanagan could do it!" They both laughed. "So what are you asking for the place, Troy?"

"I'd let it go for fifty. You have about twenty-one months left on the lease, and there's an automatic renewal option as long as you make the rent. I've never even met the landlord. The rent is eight hundred a month. That's about what you make on an average night. For fifty large you get it, quite literally lock, stock and barrel. What do you think?"

Ed had already decided what he thought.

"Well, I'm gonna have to see the place first, but yeah, so far so good. I'm interested."

"Terrific. Hold on—miss? Two Johnny Walker Blue's over here!" Turning back to Ed, "let's celebrate this thing in style."

They toasted to the deal. Then Miller continued. "Hang loose tomorrow, you can stay at my place if you want. Then I'll head up there with you this weekend and I can show you the ropes and introduce you to the manager, so called, this fucking local moron—that's a different story. First thing you should do is fire that asshole. Anyway. Miss? Two more Johnny's over here!"

And Ed felt that old familiar buzz in his head and he felt pretty good, sitting here in a new city with an old friend and (maybe) a home for the new money. He pounded the shot and many more.

***

48

Ed and Troy Miller were heading back through the Eisenhower Tunnel towards Denver. It had been a long day, and they were both quiet. Miller had shown him the bar, took him around town and introduced him to a few people. He'd spoken to a realtor about renting a house and had looked at a couple of places. There were many vacancies in town. Nothing like the lower Keys where you'd have four waiters crammed into one dead end double wide. Up there you could feel the…space.

The ball was in Ed's corner now. Everything looked kosher to him. The next day was Sunday and the plan was set. They'd meet with some of Miller's boys and tailgate at the Bronco's game.

On Monday, they would meet at Miller's attorney's office, Ed would sign the papers and become the proud owner of Paddock Enterprises LLC, D.B.A. Trapper's Bar. Miller never asked him where he got the money and Ed never told him.

Then he'd move up to Winterland. Miller would come up the first few weekends to make sure he was getting on all right and tie up any lose ends.

***

By Monday afternoon, after the smash and grab real estate job, Ed had a folder full of legal documents on the seat next to him and he drove solo up to Winterland. This was it. He had about seven thousand in cash left in the duffel bag. It was late September and he had a few weeks to figure out how to run a bar before the mountain opened. He felt grand.

***

About halfway down Fox Tail Pass, you ease around a bend and suddenly see the town, then the hill. Town begins and ends in the space of three stoplights. Main Street is lined with two story brick buildings. Behind that a brief grid of small ranches and bungalows melt back to nothing.

Main Street-alley-First Street-alley-Second Street-alley-alley-dirt road-pasture. That's about it. The businesses to the south side of town are mostly shut down. The empty cattle yards sit rusting beyond that.

As the sun sets on Winterland, Main Street looks like a checkerboard. About half the storefronts appear black. They are open for business, of which there is little. The rest are white washed and covered with newspapers. They await new business, of which there is none.

The mountain sits on the near edge of town, just below the pass, its thirty-one trails facing west. Through clear, piney air you see rust and tan colored trails sluice between green pines and white aspens, their leaves golden in the fall when snow begins to dust the upper trails.

A chairlift runs right up the gut. From the rope maze in front up to the summit building, it rises twelve hundred feet in fourteen minutes. Skirting the flanks are two rope tows and a J bar that occasionally works. Three structures dot the base area. One is the ski patrol/maintenance building. There's a rental and ski school shack and a small lodge with bathrooms, day lockers and a bar and grill.

There is a dirt parking lot. There is minimal snowmaking, there is no place to shop. There is absolutely no après ski scene.

There is, however, inexpensive skiing on a mountain that gets dumped with over 400 inches of light powder snow every winter.

Chapter Seven

It was late by the time Ed checked into the Fox Tail Pass motel. It was a simple place with twenty-four (vacant) rooms arranged around the square parking lot. In the morning he'd go speak with the realtor, then head over to the bar and check in with the manager.

The manager worried him some. Miller had gone to great lengths to explain what a completely unreliable fuck up this guy was. Indeed, the one time Miller had done a thorough inventory, it was clear that much of the booze moving through the place never made it to the bottom line. The beer sales alone should have been driving cash flows. Something was wrong. Slow or not, Miller was getting sponged.

Of course the hick who ran the place denied it, but Miller knew. But what was he gonna do? Someone had to run the place. Seventy hours a week he was down in Denver, chained to the trading desk, risking millions of dollars in the fixed income derivative market. And even if he was the titular owner, he had no time to audit some slap-ass bar.

That's where Ed hoped to make an improvement. For Miller it had been a lark, a profit move. For Ed it represented a new way of life. Starting fresh. He couldn't wait. He stared at the motel ceiling and thought of ways to improve business…the new friends he'd make…the trout he'd catch from the river. He couldn't wait to sink his teeth into this bar business. But whatever he did, it was gonna be clean and legal. No more bullshit.

***

The next day Sandy Connor drove Ed around town in her big Buick. They looked at a few places, and he finally signed the lease on a ranch on the near edge of town, close to the hill. From his back deck he had a view of the ski area.

It was a funny little town.

Most of the houses looked the same. A mixture of Alamo-style concrete bungalows and steep gabled Victorians. Most were small and austere, with little front porches and fenced in backyards neatly organized into boxes on the grid. Winterland had been settled a century ago by pragmatic Norwegians who came for the fur trade and their utilitarian style persisted in the architecture. All they required was a place to trade and a river. They built small, efficient houses that were easy to heat. A hundred years later, the town was little changed. There had been (muted) booms when fur prices soared, and busts alike. When the cattle yard came to town in '18, mostly to take advantage of lucrative trade supplying the Army with fresh beef, things had picked up. A building boomlet had followed. But even in the good years of the cattle yard, which stretched into the mid 1980's, the population had rarely climbed much past four thousand. There was just nothing to do here. Ranchers are generally a serious minded people and those who wanted to ski had a dozen easier-to-reach options before they'd hit Winterland. So the town was in a frozen state. It never grew and it didn't entirely fade.

Main Street was built wide to accommodate cattle drives. When they ended, the two story brick storefronts sat empty. The little houses tucked behind were in decline. Weeds grew tall in front of abandoned hovels.

After the cattle yard went bust the population was halved and a decade of belt-tightening ensued. Like any market correction, the highly leveraged took the worst beating. Those with low mortgages and thrifty business tended to weather the storm a bit better. But the town was a ghost of its old self. The vitality was lost.

And only now, in the late '90's, as word spread through mountain-freak culture, were there any signs of hope. Word in the parking lots and at the trailheads and white water camps was that there was a little ski town with (gasp) some affordable digs. Reportedly it wasn't huge but they got a ton of snow. Slowly the tide started to turn.

It was into this peculiar little economic twilight that Ed opened for business.

***

Greg Hamilton hoped to have the hill opened by Thanksgiving. At this elevation, on this storm track, it usually started snowing around Labor Day.

Snow was not the problem. Everything else was. Hamilton had almost unwittingly become the last remaining defender of this hill. It was not a role he anticipated. He still loved Winterland even as it ground him into chop meat.

A lifelong skier from upstate New York, he'd been a typical ski bum since he moved west in '94. Banging nails all summer to cover a season pass, he'd spent his first three winters in Breckenridge. Then a bearded tele skier on Chair 6 had told him about the fishing jobs in Valdez. How any yokel could go up there and fish for two months and walk with like fifteen-twenty grand.

So he'd signed on, green, as a deckhand on a seiner. And it was harder than he thought. Eighteen hours a day of breaking your back. But after the summer he had something like twenty one thousand dollars in cash in a backpack. He ended up at the bar, celebrating the end of the commercial season with two other ski bums. One of whom was rich and the other of whom had a great idea. Over shots they explained how they were trying to buy their own ski area. They had it all figured, they just needed one more partner who loved to ski and had a few dollars to invest, to get it off the ground. And that's how, at age twenty-five, Greg Hamilton became a limited partner in Winterland Ski Area.

And at first it was great. He put a down payment on a small house in town and his partners lived nearby and they all skied and partied together. They did a little bit of business. There were a few hundred locals who bought passes, which barely covered costs; the profits would come with the crowds. The crowds never came. It was next to impossible to get people to travel up there. They were too isolated to get day-trippers in any serious numbers and they lacked a local airport, not to mention condos that would bring in families for a ski week. The only advertising they could afford—radio time in the late night Denver and Fort Collins markets—had had no effect. The cash flow barely covered the mortgage. So forget about planned improvements and even maintenance. Everyone lost money. After one season, both partners bailed. The partnership document that Greg had signed was filled with negative covenants that he didn't understand until it was too late. He didn't want to sell so he was forced to buy them out on unfavorable terms. When finally he'd had his buddy Jake, a third year at Cornell Law, take a look at the contract, he learned how bad it really was. How if he failed to make even one debt payment, he would be personally responsible for the default. That's what the jointly liable clause meant. Further, he was contractually obligated to sell the property to the highest bidder, should one emerge. Reluctantly, though necessarily, he put the place up for sale. And there were no offers, because seemingly everyone but him knew that Winterland was a dead end. And he had done what he could to make the place better and it didn't amount to shit. With no customers, he was dead. It was difficult to pay the loan. On a good day the ski area generated about a thousand dollars and with interest he owed one million three hundred fourteen thousand. So every payment was a high stakes game of chicken. The bankruptcy would ruin him, since in the court's eyes his personal assets and liabilities and those of the ski area were inseparable. Not that he had any assets these days. He'd lost the house, sold his truck, even sold his skis (he got by with demos from the rental shop) and finally cashed in his IRA. He was flat broke, sleeping on a friend's couch.

The snow was consistent. The staffing…less so.

Word of the first Winterland all-staff meeting of the year, to take place on October first, was spread by word of mouth. Hamilton longed for a phone tree, or an email list, or some way to contact his workers quickly. It was just one more thing that made his job a twenty-four hour a day logistical nightmare. So for a few days he just made the rounds of the bars and spread the word. He called what numbers he had, sent a few emails. He didn't reach very many people and the meeting was the next day. Even at a more successful (read: every other) ski resort, turnover was high. But at Winterland? Forgetaboutit.

When summer came most of his staff scattered. White water guiding, touring, mountain biking, anything to stay active. They always left. Some of them came back. The risky decision to ignore the insurance company-mandated piss tests had helped. A little. Ideally he'd have fifteen people for base operations, ten instructors, five groomers who could drive the cats, twelve patrollers and some guys to work the parking lots. Ideally he'd have qualified mechanics to maintain the lifts, licensed carpenters to keep the lodge up, and patrollers with medical certificates. Ideally he'd have a lot of things.

There was a silver lining. Business was picking up, ever so slightly, each year, as new arrivals trickled into town. Especially now, during mud season. But it would be a while before they started to help the bottom line. With the short staffing, the long hours—eighty hours was a slow week—and the crushing debt, Hamilton could feel it slipping away. He was a tough kid who worked his ass off, but whatever reserves of strength and endurance he had, he'd used most of them up just getting through last year. This year was gonna be tough. Even living on coffee and Copenhagen, he was tired all the time. Something had to give.

***

Over at Tres Hermanas, Beth, Jen and Jen were getting ready for the season—ordering corn tortillas, California avocados, black beans, cilantro, onions, tomatoes—they served burritos so fresh that their restaurant required neither freezer nor can opener.

They'd met at Sugarbush when Beth was at Johnson State and the Jens went to Middlebury. Skipping graduation, they hit the road. After six months of selling burritos, sleeping in the van and at campgrounds and crash pads from coast to coast, following Phish around, they settled in Winterland, glad to have a home base. They'd heard about the place in Mountain View (or was it Portland?) from a white dread who'd traded them five goo balls for a couple Veggie Supremes.

So they took what was left of their graduation money, pooled their vending profits—fourteen grand, total!—and opened up shop last year on B Street, just off Main. The shop, an abandoned grain and feed store, came cheap. Their rent got them a storefront location with an apartment above it. They scrubbed for days, painted everything in sight (twice) and threw a hand made sign out front:

FIVE BUCKS FOR A BURRITO THE SIZE OF YOUR HEAD

Their first year went pretty well. And thanks more to the bargain basement rent and their road-tested propensity for thrift, rather than serving many actual customers, they'd made a small profit. They hoped this year would be even better. They knew their way around town now. They hung with the locals, drank with the ski patrol, skied with the barflies. It would be an ok year, and if they could just get a few more people to drop in, they could really take off.

Still padding around in her pajamas upstairs, Jen #1 ran the numbers, checked her math, and smiled. It was looking like a good year.

***

Frank "Jack" Hammer rolled out of bed around eleven and slipped his rattlesnake boots on over his white socks. He took a pull of Jimmy Beam before buttoning up his jeans. Hammer was a self-styled concert promoter. His business card read JackHAMMER! PRODUCTIONS! His daddy had been second in charge at the cattle yard before his untimely death. Cody Hammer had a reputation as a hard working and decent man, and Frank had spent his twenty-seven years proving that fruit can indeed fall very far from the tree.

Raised in what by the standards of a western cow town could be called upper middle class, Frank had spent most of his life coasting. A hell raising loud mouth who always knew daddy would bail him out, in high school he'd specialized in stealing beer from freshman and beating up hippies. He'd graduated (although not from high school) to larceny and minor fraud. When sober he was merely an insufferable pain in the ass. With half a load on he'd challenge anyone—provided that they were smaller and/or Hammer had backup—to a fight.

He had a job at present, which was rare. A short-term scam until a better score came along.

Of course, like a lot of things, the event and concert promotion business in Winterland was kinda slow these days. So as a sideline he sold party powder for a hundred dollars a gram.

And that went slightly better, even if he was his own best customer.

He just needed one big score this winter that could put him back on easy street. And he had an idea for what that score just might be. He did two small lines, rubbed the stubble on his chin, and pressed his cowboy hat down over his blond curls.

**

A block and a half down the alley from JackHAMMER! PRODUCTIONS! and around the corner from Tres Hermanas, in the newsroom of the weekly Winterland Wire, shouting down the phone, sat Kent Jennings, newspaperman.

Bruce Cleland, managing editor and publisher of the Wire, cautiously approached Jennings's desk. You never knew. As Cleland got closer, he overheard…

"Listen, fuck-stick, answer my question. I don't care about the fucking—what? No! The question! Jerk! Fine, look for your fucking face on the front page Thursday, asshole!" He slammed the phone down and jerked his head up at Cleland, who wished he'd chosen a different time to stop by. But with Jennings, it was almost always a bad time.

Jennings ran hot. He feared no one. And his sources were sacrosanct. Cleland, a gentleman publisher from back East, had never encountered anyone quite like him. Cleland had worked with enough writers to know that the best of the breed were sometimes a little… different. And even by that standard Jennings was a freak. He lived in a yurt with no electricity. He dressed like a buffalo hunter (including carrying a Bowie knife on his hip wherever he went) and put away single malt scotch and homemade rotgut with equal aplomb. He puked in libraries, he passed out at stoplights. But he could write like the wind. Cleland sometimes squirmed at the copy, but it always checked out. It was lively and libel proof. And it (to the extent possible in a town with about a thousand people) sold newspapers.

Jennings had come of age in the Bay Area of the 1960's. He'd graduated Berkeley—with a degree in biology of all things—and started writing soon after, if only to support his surfing habit. He'd written for a series of left wing scream sheets, partied with the Dead, and once drove three hundred miles into Mexico on a motorcycle with no brakes to buy a pizza.

When the Hell's Angels violently disrupted the Vietnam Day peace parade in '66, he was there. Indeed, *The Chronicle* ran a front-page photo of Allen Ginsberg pleading for calm amidst the mayhem. In the background you can just make out a Hell's Angel who was only prevented from stomping a teen-age girl when he was suddenly drop kicked with a boot to the skull. You don't see him in the frame, but the boot is at the end of Jennings's leg.

Since Cleland had hired Jennings the Wire hadn't seen a dull moment. Jennings's award winning "Live Wire" column ran on Thursday and was usually the talk of the town.

Jennings stared up at his boss, his eyes hot.

"Who were you just screaming at?"

"The Sheriff."

Cleland looked at the wall and shook his head, as if he'd now, finally, heard it all. "Well, that's good. We haven't had a libel suit in a while. There's a new owner at Trappers. Head over and talk to him. Sort of a 'New Faces Around Town' kind of a piece. Five hundred words. What do you say?"

"Sounds all right to me."

"And Jennings?"

"Yeah?"

"Don't stay so long you have to be carried out this time."

Jennings shrugged.

***

Earlier that day Nut Richards had reluctantly met with his finance team. Degbert dreaded the meetings now too, it was always the low point of his week. Every week he brought in new ideas, deals that would make the company money, and few of which had already started to work out. But this little ski area…whose name he would no longer even say out loud it disgusted him so. But his boss had become obsessed! Skiing held little interest for Nut, but he had some half-baked idea of building a mountaintop hideaway for him and his bimbo brigade. He always had to be first, he'd made his name as a maverick. When everyone else was drilling near Houston, who bought huge tracts (cheap!) near Permian? When oil tanked in '79, who had the biggest supply of natural gas to hedge? He been burned too, he took a bath on condos near Houston, and the stock market had not been kind to him either. And now that oilmen his age were moving to ranches near Aspen and Beaver Creek, he had to blaze the trail again. He saw it as a way to remake the broken town in his own image. He wanted to be the first big money man in Winterland. He talked of little else.

They had misinterpreted silence on the part of Winterland as a hard line negotiating stance. They had made three escalating offers to no effect. They figured the old boy knew something they didn't. The reality was that Hamilton was so busy trying to get the place open—doing interviews and wrestling with balky lift motors and parking cars and fixing the fryolator—not to mention attempting to stave off bankruptcy—that he had lost all touch with the outside world.

Degbert quickly tried to explain that while they had had absolutely no success purchasing this two-bit ski area, there were many more lucrative capital opportunities. California Wind Farms, for example.

"Could be a huge pop. Market's undervaluing the IPO by almost three points. By taking an early equity position, I think we can maximize—"

"Maximize? You best maximize that ski area. Get me in there, and I mean all the way in, or you're out on the street."

***

Jennings grabbed his Russian fur hat and headed for the door. Some fresh air would do him good. The longer he was trapped in the sterile fluorescent hum of the newsroom, the more he tended to get in trouble. He needed space. That's why he'd moved to the Rockies in the first place. He walked down the alley, turned right on C Street and right again on Main. He looked up at the hill. Snow covered the upper trails. Wouldn't be long now. Soon he was at Trapper's door.

He entered the barroom. Chairs up on tables. Dark and smelly with lemon house cleaner and stale beer. He saw a guy behind the bar.

"Can I get a double margarita?"

"Uh, we're not really open yet."

"Oh, all right. Can I get a drink while I wait?"

"Ah…sure, man. Margarita?"

"Ahh, whatever's cool with me. I'm Kent Jennings with the Wire. Are you the new owner?"

"Yeah. Ed Stallings. Nice to meet you."

58

Chapter Eight

Danny was ten miles from Fort Collins when the Subaru shit the bed. He was rolling north on I-25, checking out the mountains through the window when the head gasket blew. The car was fucked.

He got it towed to a garage that confirmed this. Estimates ranged from twenty-two hundred (to fix it) to thirty-eight hundred (for a rebuilt engine to replace it). Neither option was viable.

He decided to abandon the car before it killed him. The guy at the junkyard gave him fifty bucks for it, plus a ride to the edge of town.

Piled in the grass next to the road in the shadow of the Rockies sat Danny's gear. Just a couple backpacks, a sleeping bag and his Nalgene bottle. The rest he'd ditched. He had two bottles of wine left from the case Dab had given him.

He still wasn't even in Wyoming! Carless. Now he was just standing on the side of the road like an idiot. He had to laugh at the ridiculousness. He shook his head. Fuck it. He was glad to be rid of that fucking liability once and for all. He stuck his thumb out and hoped to catch a ride before it got dark.

***

Greg Hamilton was a staff of one. He'd taken a week off in August, then started getting the hill ready to open. Now he was behind schedule. The ticket window had been vandalized over the summer, and he needed some strapping to build a new frame. He was rummaging around behind the snowmobiles, looking for some scraps—he had long since learned the value of hanging onto things that in his previous life he would have tossed. Hence, all over the place, things were jerry rigged. An old door served as a table in the patrol shack. Chairs were whatever could be glued back together. Some rooms in the lodge had an abstract expressionist bent from when the paint ran low and color substitution became mandatory. These days he tended to hang onto things, and they accumulated in the maintenance shack, a semi-organized Quonset hut full of tires, paint cans, cans of mixed nails, ski wax, hoses, 2x4s, twine, old windows and gas cans.

As he searched for the strapping he noticed some rolled up pieces of paper on the floor by the fax machine. He meant to check them out when he was done rebuilding this window frame. But when he finished with that, Dennis Jeffries, his cook, showed up for the season. Doubling the workforce. They spent the afternoon trying to get the grill and fryolaters working.

Hamilton looked up at the hill that he loved, saw the upper trails dusted with snow, and remembered when the place filled his heart with hope.

Hamilton was on his way home after eight that night when he remembered the faxes, and made a mental note to check them in the morning. Probably just some junk mail promoting the latest K2 and Rossignol models. He was bone tired and fell asleep before nine.

***

It was almost dark when Danny saw the headlights. The car slowed. It was a navy blue Wagoneer with wood paneling. Its roof rack was loaded with bags.

"Where you headed?"

"Jackson Hole."

"All right man, gonna make some turns?"

"I guess so. I'm not very good, but yeah, I'm going there to ski."

"Hop in man. We can get you up a ways."

Two guys swung out and helped Danny with his stuff. They were about his age, dressed in t-shirts and shorts. Soon they had his stuff lashed to the rack and they all piled in. Now there were five of them.

"What's up, brah? I'm Kevin, that's my girlfriend, Meg. That's Peter and that's Brian."

"I'm Danny."

"You go to fort fun?"

"What?"

"Fort Collins, you go to CSU?"

"Oh, Colorado State, right. No, I was ah…my car broke down. I just sold it, actually. I'm actually coming through from Chicago. I'm trying to get to Jackson, but it's just been one fucking nightmare after another with that car. I've been on the road for weeks, man. Its cost me so much money."

"Harsh," said Kevin, the driver. He wore a green and gold CSU t-shirt over his lanky frame.

"Bummer dude," said Brian, the guy with dark curly brown hair. He wore green Smith Slider sunglasses and his t-shirt said Makisupa Police Department Badge 420. "Say, maybe this will revive your spirits a little." He handed Danny a joint.

"Giggin. Thanks, man." Danny lit the joint and had a nice long toke. Kevin turned the radio back up. The sun was beginning to dip behind the Rockies. Danny exhaled a plume and passed the joint to the girl. "This is terrific man. Thanks for stopping. Where are you guys headed, anyway?"

"We're skiers too. Well, Brian snowboards. But we're going up for the season. Heading out to Winterland."

***

"Where are ya from?" asked Jennings. He sat on a bar stool and lit up a Camel.

"Detroit." Ed usually said Detroit. When you answered Grosse Pointe or Bloomfield Hills, people sometimes reacted. Like you were rich. Like Ed was. Was. "But I've been living down in the Keys for a while now." And trafficking psychedelic drugs by the trunk full and committing capital fraud with illicit cash. He left that part out.

"What brought you out this way?"

"I was tired of the life down there. Drinking all the time."

"So you bought a bar?"

"Well, it's…I know, fair point. I guess I just needed a change of scenery."

"Did a geographic, as the Kiwis say."

"Yeah, a geographic. I like that. My buddy from high school works for Riggity in Denver, he sold me the place."

"Right. Tim Miller?"

"Troy Miller."

"Never got to know him."

"Yeah, I don't think he made it up here very often. He works around the clock more or less. Anyway, he wanted to get rid of the place and I was looking for something to do, so it kind of worked out. Next thing I knew—need a refill?"

"Good man."

Ed topped up the brew. "Next thing I know I signed the papers and bought this place. I literally just got in town last night. It's been an interesting few days. So tell me, what's it like here?"

Jennings chuckled. "Well…I like it. But that doesn't mean much. People here…this was a cattle town, a ranching town, for generations. Hard working Germans, Swedes, Norwegians, church folks, Protestant work ethic, all that, they were the backbone. But then the cattle yard closed, and things got tough. And stayed tough. Going on ten, twelve years now. This place is starting to go under. When I started at the Wire, we had nine in the newsroom. Now there's two of us. Things change."

"How come you stuck around?"

"Well, like I said, I like it. I'm from the Oakland. That's no place to go back to. I've gotten used to the pace of life up here. I have a little spread above town. No one fucks with me. I like having bighorn sheep wander through my property. I like the alpenglow. It's not for everyone, but it suits me."

"Say, you know anything about fishing?"

"Some."

"Great, I'd love to go fly fishing sometime. If you know any good spots."

"Yeah, I know some great spots. And I'm not gonna fuckin' waste 'em on you."

They both laughed. "Fishermen are the same everywhere. I wouldn't expect you to give up any secrets."

"I'll get you out there, once you get settled in. Biggest rainbows in the west, if you know where to look. Some cutthroat, too. Are you a skier?"

"I've never been. But I figure I'll be giving it a shot at some point."

"Might as well. One thing you can count on around here is snow up to your sack."

"Yeah, that's what I heard. I have a view of the ski area from my place. Looks nice."

"It is nice. At least, it's not bad. Nothing like Vail, terms of size, but it's an okay little lump."

"When do they open this year?"

"If they open this year."

This brought Ed up short. He'd planned on skiers being a solid chunk of his business. "Why wouldn't they open?"

"Well, times are tough. This young feller, bout your age, I suspect, bought the place a couple winters ago. And proceeded to get ass raped. His partners bailed on him, and he's on his own now. Sisyphean task. Hill never made much money anyway, it's a volunteer type situation, bust your ass to break even. He's a nice kid, but I think by the time spring rolls around the bank's gonna put him under."

"That's too bad. So let me ask you, Kent, do you know this—oh, can we do this off the record or whatever?"

"Sure."

"Do you know the guy who's been running this place for Miller?"

"Jack Ass."

"He is?"

"No, that's his name. Actually, it's Frank Hammer. He calls himself "Jack" Hammer. I call him something else. His daddy was a good man. Thinks he's promoter. Only thing that guy promotes is an argument for euthanasia."

"What's his deal?"

"His deal is he's a fucking retard."

"Miller thought he was maybe dipping in the till."

"Yeah, dipping his balls in the till, more like. Jack Ass'd steal anything that wasn't nailed down. If I were you I'd offer him an early retirement package. You wanna make any money in this place, and I'll say this on the record, you're not gonna do it with him hanging around."

***

Music played in the dark cab while the Wagoneer climbed and climbed. They were approaching the top of Fox Tail Pass, and the transmission rarely left second gear. Danny felt extremely comfortable, and it wasn't just the joint.

"Where's the turnoff? Somebody wake dip shit."

Pete tugged one of the stocking feet that hung over the back seat. "Hey man, where's this camping spot?"

Brian exhaled and stirred. His sunglasses hung crazily off his face. "After you pass the sign for the Continental Divide, it's the first turnoff on the right."

Soon they passed the carved wooden sign demarcating America into Atlantic and Pacific watersheds. The headlights swung off the paved road and up the steep and narrow dirt track into the woods. Kevin shifted down into first and they jounced up, up, up, Danny's head occasionally hitting the roof. Suddenly the trail flattened out and they popped out of the trees into a grassy meadow.

"Good a place as any," said Kevin, coasting to a stop.

Danny's eyes were wide. He bounded out of the Jeep. Grass brushed his khakis, covered his Samba classics. Kevin turned off the motor and Danny looked around in the sudden quiet darkness of the broad plateau. Bright stars overhead felt just out of reach.

The rest piled out of the Jeep slowly, stretched, and started to make camp. Brian crawled out of the back, still wrapped in a comforter. After they staked out tents, they dispersed into the woods to gather ground fall for a fire. Meg did a little yoga as Pete got the Coleman stove fired up and started a pot of water for pasta. Danny took a walk to the far edge of the meadow, where jagged boulders marked the western edge of the Pass. He scrambled up on a big rock. He looked out over more mountains than he'd ever seen. Danny felt the cool, clean air on his face.

By the time he wandered back to the group, supper was almost ready.

"Hungry dude?"

"Are you kidding? I almost ate a pine cone over there."

Pete hacked up a big onion and smashed a few cloves of garlic, then dumped them into the pot with a handful of pepper and doused the whole thing with a jar of red sauce. They ate from bowls by the still-catching bonfire.

On camping chairs and coolers they ate in comfortable silence. Danny uncorked his penultimate bottle of wine.

"To new friends. Thanks for picking me up."

'You got it, brah."

"Here, here."

The wine slowly circled the group.

After dinner, Kevin sat on the tailgate and rolled a bomber. Danny volunteered to wash the dishes.

The vibes were comfortable.

While Danny scrubbed up, Meg dragged a black case off the roof. She pulled out a baby Taylor six string and started to tune up.

Soon the dishes were done and they were back around the fire. The night air was cool. It was very dark. Pete had thrown a fleece over his checked shirt and Brian had his wooly Burton hat pulled low. The fire sparked. Meg looked up at the stars, dreamily, her head rolling back and forth, and Danny just fell in love with her…with them…with the whole scene.

"So is this place any good, or what Kevin?"

"Hey man, I spoke with Framingham; he said it's the shit."

"How great could it be? I've barely even heard of this place, Wintertown."

"Winter*land*."

"I've *never* heard of it, and I've been in Colorado since freshman year."

"I know, it's out there, but supposedly it's…ok, from what Framingham told me, and I checked it out, it's not huge, its barely the size of a single chairlift at Vail. But they get hella snow and you can rent a house on the mountain for like no money."

They nodded. They were veteran couch surfers. Dirt bag skiers who knew the sights and smells of a week on the floor. Like all low rent adrenaline junkies who were willing to trade creature comforts for powder (and used to extortionate resort town rents) they could smell a bargain through a freshly painted door.

"It's chill. I drove up on Labor Day," continued Kevin. "Clocked it. And it's true, the rents are ridiculous. We should have our pick of places, right near the hill. There isn't much of a town, it's not gonna be like Breckenridge, party wise, but you can afford to fucking live there, which will be a nice change."

"Man, I hope they get *dumped* on. I'm *jonesing* to make some turns in the pow-pow."

They all nodded in silent assent. A quiet moment.

"So tell us, hitchhiking stranger, what brought you out here?"

Danny looked at Kevin, hopeful that he hadn't been caught staring at Meg. Kevin's face was open, alert, smiling. No worries.

"Well, I saw this film. And I—I'm gonna need a drink for this story, hold on." He went back to his bag and grabbed the last bottle of Chateauneuf-du-Pape, then returned to the circle, where he sat on the end of a blue Coleman cooler. He uncorked the wine with his fake Swiss army knife, took a long tug and passed it to the left. He blew out his breath. All eyes on him.

"I was tending bar, this was in Chicago. And I was feeling sort of…trapped, or something. Rat race, all that. Anyway, I was staying with a friend of mine who has a fat pad in Lincoln Park. Hipster heaven. It was cool. Anyway, I was kicking back one morning,"—the joint came to him, he inhaled deeply and passed it on—"and I saw this DVD on the table. OK? I had never seen it before, but it looked…it had a cool cover, it was called "Grass Roots." And I had no idea what it was, but I put it on. It was this ski film by these guys called Wyoming Cliff Posse."

"Oh, WCP."

"Those guys are sick!"

"So, you've heard of them?"

65

"They're fucking legends up in J-Hole. You'll probably see them when you get up there."

"Yeah, check any bar around last call."

"Yeah, or at ten a.m." They all laughed.

"Yeah, so you know about these guys? I had never heard of them. So I just threw on the disc, no expectations, you know? And it just caught me *out*. Guys flying off cliffs, snow up to their armpits, snow going right over their fuckin' head. It is like *that deep*. I've never seen anything like it. The music was cool. The fucking scene was cool. And in that moment I knew that if I did anything the rest of my life, I had to try that shit. So I mean, I quit the next day. That was it. Packed up my car—my fucking car! What a joke. I hate that piece of shit! Anyway, that nightmare is over. So I start driving out, I had a few bucks saved at that point, but the car from hell bleeds all of my duckets, I finally ditch it while I still have a dollar to my name. I started hitching…and now here I am…with you dudes."

"That's awesome, man. Well, we're glad to have ya," said Kevin.

"No doubt," said Brian. Meg smiled beatifically.

"Well, Jackson rocks, there's no question. You're gonna love it. I went there once on spring break. Steep. But its big money, too, like eighteen hundy for a pass. You end up working three jobs just to live there. That's why we're gonna check out Winterland. It's just the other side of the pass. We'll be there in the morning."

Eighteen hundred for a pass? Danny almost shit himself. He wasn't even sure if he had that much left, total. Plus he still had to buys skis, find a place to live…

Meg plucked a few strings, adjusted the tuning pegs, and plucked again. They all turned to watch. She was willowy and blond and ethereal. Even in her t-shirt and tie dyed skirt, even in her muddy hiking boots, she was feminine. Danny realized he had the wine again, and he went to take a sip. Whoa. Almost fell when he leaned back. Steady on, boy, steady on. He gathered himself. He took a breath. He was all right. Better than all right.

He looked up at the stars, at the fire, at the intent faces of the boys around him, all eyes on Meg now. Softly she started to strum a few chords, her thin fingers gliding on the fret board.

Chapter Nine

Danny awoke in the weird orange light of daybreak through a tent wall. He stirred around and noted traces of a hangover. He had to piss.

He wriggled from his sleeping bag, unzipped the tent and crawled out into the morning dew. The air was cold. In the distance he saw Meg in an inverted handstand, with her legs stretched in a diamond shape. As he passed the big tent, Danny could hear snoring.

He walked to the edge of the trees. His piss steamed from the tall grass. Walking back towards camp, he bent and wiped his hands in the dewey tall grass, then rubbed the coolness on his face, washing away the night. His clothes smelled like smoke.

He looked around the plateau, much smaller in the daylight. But the colors! Wildflowers carpeted the meadow running up towards an escarpment, which abruptly turned up and topped out with scabrous, fang-like boulders. The sun rose through the aspens to the east, long shadows dappled the meadow. He went back to his boulder from last night and looked out over the mountains. Sharp peaks like white caps on Lake Michigan. Hills stretched away to the north and west, the sun wrapping around the peaks and flooding the valleys between. Piney smells of earth on the misty meadow.

"I love this," he found himself saying aloud. "I love this."

When he wandered back towards the tents everyone was stirring. Brian shivered a little as he revived the fire from the ashes. Kevin cut quite a figure wearing only unlaced logging boots, red long john bottoms and a cowboy hat.

"Mornin Danny."

"Hey, good morning. How'd everyone sleep?"

"Great man. You want some pancakes?"

"Giggin."

Pete whipped up some instant batter. He had the fire going and a big cast iron fry pan was starting to smoke in the middle of it. Meg walked back into camp holding the bottom of her shirt out.

"I picked some berries over there. They're a little tart, but they're good."

Pete grabbed a handful and tossed them into the already bubbling pancake in the skillet.

As pancakes came ready, Pete just handed them off. You got one, rolled it up and ate it. No mess.

They broke camp and got back in the car. Soon they were bouncing down the dirt track toward the two lane. It was almost seven a.m.

***

The first time Ed woke up on the floor of his rental house he decided he needed some furniture. He was opening Trappers nights, but few came in. He was using this downtime for a crash course in bar ownership. From the beer taps to hooking up the soda syrup to dealing with the distributor to the correct ingredients for a Tom Collins, he was learning on the fly. He planned a grand opening in a few weeks, when he'd been assured there would be more people in town. He was glad for the relative down time.

Jennings had stayed late, giving Ed his take on the town and many of its featured players. Who could help and who to avoid.

Ed had to hand it to the guy. After two margaritas, he'd easily drained fifteen pints of Fat Tire ale and only wobbled slightly when he walked out after eleven. Ed had refused his offer to pay for the drinks, hoping to gain an ally. Jennings knew everything.

Ed had a glass of tap water for breakfast. He left the Pathfinder in the driveway and walked the three blocks to town. Many of the little houses had for sale signs out front. Others had curtains flapping through busted out windows. He found Gibbo's on Main between B and C streets. Inside, booths down the right, a row of round, flat stools ran along the pale green Formica counter on the left. Open kitchen. Ancient waitress. He had coffee with several refills, eggs over medium, bacon and toast.

"More coffee, hun?"

"Sounds great. Say, do you know any place that sells furniture around here?"

"Talk to Gus Woodrie. He's got a place on D Street. Not exactly a furniture showroom, but he sells a bit of everything."

"That sounds great. Say, I'm Ed Stallings. I just bought Trappers. Stop by sometime."

"My honky-tonkin days are over, hun."

Ed paid, walked up Main and turned right. D Street marked the western edge of town, and the mostly boarded up shops here, which overlooked much of the rusty cattle pens, felt even more abandoned than the rest of town. Eerily quiet at this (at any) hour. He almost walked past Gus's. That's what the faded black and white painted sign out front said, in its entirety. Gus's.

Twin show windows bracketed the door, which was locked. Ed stepped back and looked at the displays. A toaster, a violin, many stuffed animals.

He put his hand over his eyes to shield the light and peer inside the shop. Inside he saw the old fella almost in his face. The guy was like a bearded bowling ball. Smiling, he unlocked the door.

"Oh, sorry to bother you, are you open?"

"If you're buying, I'm open. Come on in. I'm Gus Woodrie. Nicetameetcha."

"I'm Ed Stallings. I own Trappers. And I need some furniture. They told me at Gibbo's that this was the place to check."

"Well, come on in and take a look."

Gus flipped on a few lights. Ed looked around. It was like a shop from the 1930's or something. Old but neat, dimly lit but cozy. It was a cross between a goodwill store, a pawnshop and a used farm equipment show.

"Can I get you a cup of tea?"

"No, I'm fully caffeinated. Thanks though."

A cat hopped onto the counter. Gus was friendly. He had a long beard. Ed noted a few missing teeth. They chatted for a bit, while Ed looked around. A bit of everything was for sale. Some stuff was new, some stuff was from the New Deal.

"This is some collection you have here."

"I started out selling radios. Course this was when radios had vacuum tubes and took two guys to move em. When people started to move on, I ended up with a lot of estate sales, donations, whatever. I like to think of this stuff as museum remnants of the better days."

Ed picked out a table and chairs, a bookshelf, an incomplete set of dishes and several large paintings. Gus asked one hundred-twenty and Ed gave him two bills, keep the change. Gus didn't have a bed for sale, but suggested Ed try the motel. One place lead to another and by early afternoon Ed had introduced himself at shops, private homes and one garage. Buying this and that. For ten bucks, for forty bucks. By three he had most of a house crammed into (and onto) the Pathfinder.

Ed unpacked, then went down to the bar at four. He found Hammer waiting out front.

"My key doesn't work."

"I know, I changed the locks," said Ed.

"Well, I'm gonna a new key. Pronto."

"Yeah, that's what I wanted to talk to you about. Why don't we go inside?"

Ed unlocked the bolt and Hammer followed him into the dark barroom.

***

The Wagoneer careened down the steep blacktop, descending the eight and nine percent grades on the west end of Fox Tail Pass. Even in first gear, the tires were squealing around corners. They passed a runaway truck ramp.

"What's that?"

"That's for when a big semi hauling whatever loses its brakes. They can use the runaway truck ramp to eat their speed."

Danny looked at the ramp as they sped past it. It was just a gully carved into the hillside, with a massive pile of small gravel, the size of a house, at the end. It didn't look like a very hospitable option, but he supposed it was better than flying off the side of the hill at 70 mph. No joke, out here.

Kevin was tense at the wheel.

Danny noticed that on many curves the entire mountain dropped away from the road's edge. He said, "you'd think they'd build guardrails."

"They can't. They wouldn't be able to push snow over the edge, and the pass would close," said Brian.

"It would shut down for months, probably all winter," said Meg.

Danny thought about rolling off the side of the mountain. There were many sketchy switchbacks.

The automatic transmission whined in protest of first gear. The engine cooling light came on. The car started to overheat. Down, down, down they went. Kevin occasionally nursed, and occasionally stomped, the brakes.

And this was bare, warm pavement. Danny imagined an iced over mid-winter descent and shuddered. They came around a bend and saw the ski area.

"Thar she blows."

"It's beautiful."

"That's our new home boys."

"What a piece a shit."

"Come on Pete, give it a chance. Wait til you're waist deep in the pow-pow."

Danny looked at the green lift towers, the chairs hung on the main cable. The shacks at the base. Even to him the place looked small. But the mountain was beautiful, awash in bright yellows and reds.

They came to the first stoplight in town and waited, then pulled over to the tall curb and parked. With no frame of reference, they simply got out and started to walk. In ten minutes they'd walked up one side on Main Street and down the other. Kevin and Meg ducked into the first realtor they came to and shook hands with the dude. Pete, Brian and Danny continued on to Gibbo's and sat in a booth near the back.

There they lingered over coffee freefills and Danny listened to their duct taped tales.

"So me and Framingham, this was like '92, in Breck. We'd already been banned from the lodge for table grazing."

"What's table grazing?" asked Danny.

"That's where you cruise the lodge, waiting for some big family to finish their meal. The trick is you get to the table after they leave but *before* the busboy."

"Yeah, lot of times you can get half a pizza or some fries."

"But the lodge, they hate it. They think like it's bad for business."

"Right. So anyway, we get busted by the manager. I'm just gonna stay and take the rap, like what can they really do? Double secret probation, you know? But Framingham panics! He fucking bolts! The manager tried to run the okey-doke. He has some guys set up at the door, they were waiting for us, like they're gonna block us in? So Framingham goes out an open window onto the deck. But the deck stairs are blocked off too. He sees we're cut off. Everyone's skis are like lined up on the railing, so he throws two skis off the deck and he's about to jump over after them. But they weren't his skis! Some guy shouts, 'Hey! My skis!' So Framingham throws some more skis over, then jumps. There were all these tourons out there, one minute they're eating lunch, the next minute they have this wavering six-foot lunatic stealing their shit. People are like leaning over the deck now, trying to see what happened, one lady screams 'he's dead!' But Framingham shakes it off and hops up. He clicks into his skis and just drops into the trees, screaming. He's 5000. He's gone."

"What happened to you?"

"Well, now the manager is *pissed*. He comes running at me. I mean running. I end up going over the top, too."

"You dove off the deck?"

71

"I had to. Framingham threw my skis off before his."

After an hour of stories like this Kevin and Meg came back.

"All right, we've got three cribs to check out. The realtor hipped me to a few things, you can rent anything in this town, it's ridiculous. I have one in mind, but I'll let the group decide, democracy and shit."

They spent another hour checking the places out. One was clearly superior. It was a green and white Victorian on B Street. Not huge, but it had many small rooms and nooks and alcoves and closets. Four bedrooms and a nice backyard with a big shed in one corner. It was just a block from Main Street and had plenty of parking, plus a washer-drier in the basement. The rent would be less than a buck fifty apiece. There was no lease, they just had to pay first and last. They moved in that afternoon.

Danny helped them load their gear. Kev went out to get some beer and pizzas. By now it was afternoon and Danny wanted to get on the road. It was still a long ways to Jackson. But…that fire didn't seem burn so brightly now. He thought…all he wanted to do, the only reason he came out west, really, was to ski powder, and supposedly this place got that in spades. He didn't know anyone in Jackson, and here, at least, he knew these people. But still, Jackson was his stated goal…

"Hey, Kevin, just wanted to thank you again for picking me up last night. I think I'm gonna get moving. I want to get up to J-Hole." Even as he said it he felt conflict. He liked these people. Plus he wasn't sure about the money, getting up there with no car…

"Yeah, no problem, brah."

Kevin and Meg exchanged a look.

"Hey, if you're ever in town again, look us up. Always a couch waiting for you here."

Danny felt a surge of—

"Thanks man, I appreciate it. Same thing, if you're ever up in Jackson Hole, give me a shout."

He grabbed his bags and headed out. He walked the three blocks to the western edge of town and stuck out his thumb.

***

Greg Hamilton's alarm went off early. He dragged himself out of bed, downed some coffee and threw in a dip of Copenhagen. He put on his Carhart jacket and started for the hill.

He was chipping some flakes off tower one, which badly needed repainting, when he remembered the faxes. So he took a break, had a slug of water from the gallon jug at his feet and headed over to the maintenance shack.

He picked up the curled papers and flattened them out on the plywood counter. Sure enough, mostly promos announcing the new expansion at Vail, the revolutionary new shaped skis from Volkl. Then he saw page six of an official looking document from the Galveston & Colorado Ski Partners, LLC. Holy shit, is this—

It took a few moments to put the pages in order, but it sure looked like—

An offer! The lifeline that he thought would never arrive.

There were three offers, actually, dated within a week. Five weeks ago. But they kept going up! He noticed that they all had 72-hour expiry dates, but he hoped like fuck they were still interested. He ran back to the offices and started to dial.

"Richards Oil, can I help you."

"May I speak to Mr. Richards?"

"Mr. Richards is in a meeting, can I take a message?"

"Sure, tell him that Greg Hamilton called, from Winterland Ski Area."

"Please hold, Mr. Hamilton." She put him right through.

Chapter Ten

Hammer sensed trouble. When Ed closed the little plywood half door, keeping him from behind the bar—never mind the office—he figured it wasn't good. But what did this jerk know? He couldn't prove shit.

"Look, Jack. I just can't keep you on."

"But I'm the bar manager. You could use my help getting set up."

"Yeah, I know, and seriously, I want to thank you for your help. You're welcome to come down here for a drink, but I'm gonna run the place myself."

"I think you're making a big mistake. I had some plans to bring in some big acts, too. You know I run a promotion business."

"I know. I'm sorry man."

"You're gonna want to be careful Ed. I know a lot of people in this town."

(Yeah, and they all think you're a piece of shit.)

"I know man, but when Miller had this place that was one thing, he was down in Denver all the time. This is my place now. I'm gonna be here every day. And I'm just not gonna need a manager." (And I'm not gonna need anyone stealing cases of booze and selling them out the back door. And I'm not gonna need anyone selling cocaine in matchbooks over the bar. Or looking through the hole in the ladies toilets.) "I think it's for the best. Like I said, the next time you come down I'll buy your first drink, on the house."

"Fuck you, you fucking pretty boy faggot! I heard about you. I think you're a fucking queer!"

Ed couldn't believe it. It was like dealing with an angry seventh grader.

"I think you should probably go."

"I'm gonna shut this place down. I'm gonna own this fucking bar." Hammer stormed out, knocking over chairs as he went.

***

Danny sat on his backpack on the western edge of town. Perhaps once an hour a truck blew past, accelerating after the final stoplight in town. None gave him a second look.

***

Greg Hamilton listened to a few minutes of muzak while he waited for this Harlan Richards to come on the line. He ran numbers in his head... he still owed Wells Fargo one-point...three(?) million, he thought. He hadn't checked in a few days. He'd only *just* made September's mortgage payment and now there wouldn't be any cash flow until the hill opened. He *might* have enough in the company account to survive until then.

"This here's Nut Richards."

"Hi, Mr. Richards, I'm Greg Hamilton from the Winterland Ski Area. I just got your faxes."

"You *just got*...well, hell (wail hail) I musta sent them...forget all that. I figured you're a business man, and I speck you know the value of your business. But in any business, there's some potential for profit and some potential for loss. I'm in the oil business myself." (I'm inna owl bidness, muhself.)

"Are you from Texas?"

"Son, I am Texas."

Hamilton couldn't believe this guy.

"And one thing we like here in Texas is a bit of space. To stretch out in. I deal in oil. If you buy any petroleum distillate products in the southwest United States, there's a good chance you bought em through my company, you understand? I've had a good life, son, a good run. And now that I'm getting on in years, I might could use a place to call a second home. I wanna build me a ranch with an airstrip, have a nice spread. That brings me to your place. I'm looking to buy this ski area, and modernize it with some friendly development, some local jobs, create a little infrastructure up there. And course, you ask anyone who's done business with me, they'll tell you (thale tail yeww) that I know how to take care of my partners (muh pardners) so that everyone benefits. So we'd be prepared to offer you 'bout one point two million dollars for your spread there. That's for the whole shootin' match."

"Your last offer was one point three-five."

"Well, hell (wail hail) I don't have my chief financial guy, Degbert, here with me right this minute, so I'm gonna have ta talk to him and review where we're at, get current on this deal. But let's just say this,

76

are you looking to sell, 'fore I get all caught up in this offer? I'm a busy man, Mr. Hamilton."

Hamilton was beyond interested, he was desperate. Indeed he was contractually obligated to sell to the highest bidder. He just hoped to get out from under that debt. He could have kissed the big Texan. "I might be interested."

"Well, that's good. Tell you what I'll do, I'll have a meeting with my finance people, we'll prepare a tender offer and have it to you within twenty-four hours. Sound good?"

"Sounds good, I'll await your offer."

Hamilton fought to slow down. He'd offered one-point-three! That would probably make the nut. Heck, if he could crow bar another hundred grand out of the guy he could buy a condo. He didn't give a shit, he'd flip burgers for a living, if he could just get that fucking debt off his neck. Hamilton tried to get back to chipping paint, but it was hard to concentrate. This could be it. He knocked off early and decided a cold beer sounded pretty good.

***

Ed spent the rest of the afternoon doing inventory. Totally out of Jack, Jim Beam and Captain Morgan. Dangerously low on Absolut and Tangueray. He did however, have entirely too much Crème de Cacao. Like, cases of it. By what was left, he could deduce what Hammer was selling out the back, and what he wasn't. The wine was all right, several cases of that—Miller said that never sold anyway—and the beer kegs were mostly full. Through his four taps he sold Fat Tire, Alpenglow, Oasis and Budweiser. Coors Light, Amstel and Heineken by the bottle. He'd keep it simple for now. He was learning everything on the fly. The first time he'd gone to change the Coke syrup he'd gotten sticky goo all over his hands. The number he had for the distributor didn't work. The kegs were simple enough, he'd changed enough of them at Chapel Hill. If only they'd let him major in that.

He swept up a bit, then opened around six.

It was the busiest night he'd had yet.

***

For lack of any other place to go, Danny sat by the side of the road all afternoon. Perhaps ten cars passed him. None had so much as slowed down. Kev's crew had offered a couch to crash on, but the first night? It seemed like too much.

As they hours passed Danny thought about Jackson Hole. He'd had time to count his money, he was down below twelve hundred. So right there he didn't have enough to buy a season pass. And he still didn't have skis, so right out of the gate he was behind. Meanwhile he thought about Winterland. Kevin had raved about how cheap it was. Hell, if these guys could afford it…guys who prefer to eat discarded food than to work… maybe twelve hundy wasn't such a bad nest egg around here. Course, there didn't seem to be a whole lot going on in this town, in terms of jobs or whatever.

He wasn't sure what to do, but it was almost dark and he wasn't gonna sit by the side of the road any longer. He shouldered his bags and walked back into town.

He thought a few drinks would ease his mind. Halfway through the three blocks he came across a bar called Trappers. The only other place that was open and self-evidently sold alcohol was an Elks club that looked too depressing for words. Trappers it was. He walked in and took a stool at the bar.

***

Ed was moving around on the sticky black mats behind the bar, grabbing a few more cups for that pitcher, opening two Coors lights, turning the lights down, the music up.

"What can I get for you?"

"I'll take aaaaaaah…Fat Tire," said Danny.

Ed poured the draft—too much head, again, but better—and set it on the bar. "Three dollars please."

Danny walked around the barroom and sipped his pint. A few tables up front. Near the bathrooms, a pool table; couple of ratty couches in the back. It was clearly decorated from the Paul Bunyan on Acid Collection. A few of the stools were just varnished logs. Black paint had been slopped over everything. It had a certain minimalist appeal. Signed John Elway jersey behind the bar. Faded poster of a hockey player with a jersey like the Colorado state flag. Framed photos along the wall… Coors Field Opening Day 1995, Stein Erickson, Pat Schroeder.

Funky little place. Danny fancied a pool game, put his quarters on the table, and sat back at the bar to wait. He ordered another beer. The guy behind the bar seemed harried, which was funny, because the place was dead. Danny thought this guy wouldn't last five minutes at the Elephant.

He ordered another Fat Tire—which tasted even better than the first—and the guy forgot to charge him for it. Then some hippy chick ordered a Long Island Iced Tea, and he watched the guy botch it.

Ed went to pour an Oasis, but the tap spit foam on his shirt. Time to change the keg. But then two more orders came in.

At length he stopped back in front of Danny.

"You need another one?"

"Ahh..yeah, might as well."

Ed placed the brew on the bar. "Three dollars."

"You didn't get me for the last one."

"Right, six dollars. Thanks."

"No worries. Listen man, I'm not trying to call you out here, but a Long Island is vodka, gin, tequila, rum, all your white spirits, in other words, plus some triple sec and a splash of soda."

"Really? No sour mix?"

"Not usually. And that dude asked for a Manhattan, which never has gin."

"Are you a bartender?"

"I was. In Chicago."

"Oh, no shit? I'm from Detroit."

"Nice. How long you been out here?"

"Be honest with ya, I literally just bought this bar and moved here in the last week. It's been interesting."

"Pitcher of Oasis over here?"

"Coming up. Excuse me. I'm Ed by the way."

"Danny."

Ed angled the pitcher under the tap and pulled the handle. *Pfffpftt.* Still kicked. He went to go change it, then heard the phone ringing in the office.

And as it grew busier around him, Danny felt that old feeling.

"Say man, you need a hand back there?"

"Uh..yeah. Yeah, you wanna change that keg while I get the phone?"

"Giggin."

Ed went back to the office.

"Trappers."

Heavily slurred, "you fucking…faggot…I'm gonna fucking take you…out…I'm gonna own that…shit…hole…"

"Yeah, thanks for calling. Have a nice day." Ed hung up.

What was this guy's deal?

He was turning to go up front when the phone rang again.

"Trappers."

"Don't you fuckin hang—I'm gonna fuckin—"

"Hammer! Shut the fuck up!"

Ed slammed the phone down, then took it off the hook and went up front.

He found Danny behind the bar. Everyone's drinks were full. He was pouring an Oasis draft.

"Thanks for your help, man."

"You got it. Who was on the phone?"

"Oh, this…well, the old manager here, actually. I just fired him and he's not taking it very well."

"Say man, you need some help around here? I have some pretty good experience, I practically ran a place in Chicago. You're new, and I mean, maybe we could work together, get this place up and running."

Ed couldn't think why not.

"You got it, bro." They shook hands. "You wanna start tonight?"

"I can, but…let me just take care of one thing first. Can I check you in like half an hour?"

"Sure."

***

"Hey, look who it is. Pete, Meg, Danny's back. Come on in."

Danny went into the kitchen, where they were putting away canned goods and cereal from grocery bags.

"How was Jackson Hole?" asked Kevin.

"Oh, it was fat. Listen, I just got offered a job here in town. Tending bar at Trappers. And I was thinking, I don't know, maybe hang around for a bit. So I mean, would your offer still stand?"

"You want to crash out here for a while?"

"If you have the space."

"I think we do. This house has closets for its closets," said Kev.

"And it never hurts to have a friend who tends bar," called Pete from the couch.

"As long as you guys don't mind?"

"We'd love to have you Danny," beamed Meg. And that sealed it. His trip was over. A smile slowly spread across his cherubic face. "Giggin."

***

Back at the bar, Ed poured another shot for the dude with the reddish hair. It was his fifth, plus some beers.

"Celebrating tonight?"

"Yeah, man. I got some good news today. Potentially good, anyway."

"What happened?"

"I think I found a buyer for the hill?"

"Oh, no shit? You own Winterland?"

"Yeah, Greg Hamilton, nice to meet ya. You just start here?"

"Yeah, I'm the new owner, actually. Ed Stallings, nice to meet you, too."

"What happened to Miller?"

"Miller is a buddy of mine, from high school actually. He wanted out. Here I am."

"Well, sounds like we both have something to celebrate. Can I buy you a shot?"

And just before he said yes, Ed realized that he hadn't had a drink the whole time he'd been in town. And something about that felt…all right. He surprised himself when he declined.

"I'm gonna pass for now, but thanks. Hey, let me buy you your next drink. You must be psyched. I heard it's been a struggle over there. No offense."

"Yeah, it's been rough. I went into this with my eyes wide. But I had no idea things would get so bad."

"Yeah, I was talking to Kent Jennings, he said you got dicked over by some shady partners?"

"I don't know if they were shady or I was naïve, but I got stuck with the place because I thought I could make it work. It was great at first, but now…just goes to show, nice guys finish last."

"At least you're out now, right?"

"Seems like it. I have some big Texan…you should hear this guy talk. He wants to buy the place and take it big. Course, that's what I wanted to do too. I think he'll find out what I learned the hard way. Nobody wants to come here to ski. Might as well open on Pluto."

"So it's just dead, huh? Even in winter time?"

"That's what's so frustrating. The hill does make money…it breaks even. I've tried everything, promotions, radio ads, there's just no upside. I sell season passes for two-ninety nine. I can't go any lower than that. And I sell a few hundred, and the day pass is thirty-five bucks. We did a buck-a-trail promotion last year. Nothing matters. There are just not

81

enough people willing to come out this far. Its only starting to change now, but it looks like it's gonna be too late for me."

"So you're saying I picked the wrong town to buy a bar."

"No, actually, this place has always done well. Everything else is shut down. It's this or the Elks, and most people who go there are four hundred years old. You're the only game in town, and when the ski bums come back they'll come in here, don't worry. This is their watering hole. And the funny thing is last year was the busiest season they've had here in years. More people are moving to town all the time. I feel like in a couple of years this town might be up and coming again, especially if this guy Richards starts putting money into it like he says he will. This might be the perfect time to start a business here. I just can't take anymore. Bank's been on me like a Somalian on a Big Mac."

"That's good man, hopefully you can get a good price. I hope it picks up in here, it's been pretty slow."

"It's mud season. Wait til the hill opens. Hopefully by then I'll be the former owner." And he downed his shot.

Ed gave him a refill, then topped up his beer. "That's on me."

"Thanks."

***

Soon Danny came back, followed by his new roommates, who drank up a storm. The pool table stayed busy all night. Ed let Danny run the bar, amazed at his efficiency. He was short and stocky, and while he never seemed to hurry, he was almost always in motion, refilling this, emptying that. Somehow everyone's drink stayed full and money kept pouring into the till.

A few people were trickling in, so Ed went up front to check ID's. Around eleven three pretty young women came in.

"Vermont, huh? What are you doing out here?"

"Ripping pow-pow."

"I think you came to the right town."

"I'm Jen. This is Beth and that's Jen."

"Nice to meet you, I'm Ed Stallings." He was psyched. He hadn't seen very many young women in town. "I'm the new owner, at your service."

"Awesome," said Beth, the one with thick brown curls and freckles. "We just opened a burrito shop."

"We're Tres Hermanas."

82

"Oh, I think I saw your sign. On B street. Great, well, you're always welcome in here."

"Nice, and you'll have to stop by for a burrito."

"Best in town."

"It's a plan. Well, come on in. That's Danny, he's the new bartender. You tell him your first round is on me, ok? Any thing you guys need, just ask."

Soon Pete and Brian were running the pool table, taking all comers until Beth and Jen # 2 knocked them off. Hamilton was buying shots for people, and Danny was making everyone laugh. Meg looked great in her baggy wool sweater, she and Kev lounged on the couches in the back, leaning on one another. Danny pumped the jukebox with his tip quarters and Johnny Cash and the Tennessee Three filled the air with their boom-chicka-boom.

Jennings stopped by ten minutes before last call and managed to down seven drinks. The bar was less than a quarter full, but it was still the busiest night so far. Mud season was almost over. Outside it started to snow.

***

The next morning before six Ed was shivering in the Arapahoe River. Just below the train bridge, past the cattle yards, out beyond the edge of town, he double checked the zipper on his chest waders. He pulled his fleece top down tight and adjusted his ski hat. He was still cold.

This was the spot Jennings had recommended, right? More used to sight casting for tarpon and bonefish on the khaki flats, the big gray water of a boulder-filled river was new to him. He found a flat rock where his wading boots could gain purchase and set up, the water running by just at his crotch. He attached a Clauser and paid out the tapered leader, wetting the fly for weight. Then he began the rhythmic ten-to-two motion with the fly rod, loading, loading, paying out line, loading. Whoosh! He laid out the fly for presentation. A bit of a splash, not bad, but enough to spook a suspicious tarpon. He reminded himself that this was fast moving water, little splashes that spooked fish on the flats wouldn't matter here.

He began a halting retrieve and soon had the fly back within a leader's length. He whipped it back and forth, loading, and set her out again.

Ahhhhhhh…

Nice to be on the water again. It had been long weeks since he'd wet a line, and he felt the weight melt off his shoulders. Relaxing.

83

Focusing. Just him and the rod and the water. Cleansing his thoughts, rinsing his consciousness.

He forgot about the bar. He forgot about Hammer, and what a douche he was. He forgot about how he knew almost no one in this strange little western town on the edge of nowhere. None of it mattered, he felt like he was free again. Doing his own thing, something that mattered. As long as he didn't have to—he felt a tug. Easy, don't over react. Let the hook set itself, easy, easy…the line popped slack. Just a branch. He retrieved the line and started to cast again, loading, loading. Whip-whap-whip-whap. Paying out line. At ease.

Chapter Eleven

NEW YEARS EVE 1998
    "Trappers. Eight-fifty."
    She handed him a ten.
    "Keep the change."
    "Thanks, you folks have a good night."
    They piled out of the cab—
    —only to—
    "What the hell is this?"
    —a line?
    You couldn't even see Trapper's door from the street. Seemed like the whole town had turned up. A critical mass of shuffling hiking boots, corduroy, Spyder tops, Patagonia, duct taped jackets, cowboy hats worn un-ironically, ski hats, baggy pants, beards, beads, Carhart jackets, TGR t-shirts, Burton sweaters, John Deere hats, one Green Bay Packers jacket, mittens, down vests…formed an impatient line to get in. Pushing edged shoving and some time after eleven Pete just said the hell with it. A veteran of many a frat house basement scrum/siege, he could sense the crowd was ready to rumble. So in a gesture of half drunken magnanimity he let them all in at once, swamping an already busy bar.

    Inside, the room was highly decorated. Kind of. Well, the kind of look you might achieve if you planted some dynamite in a box full of decorations and lit the fuse and dove behind something heavy. Boom! Decorations.

    Brightly colored streamers and balloons hung loosely from black pipes and ductwork, making the ceiling that much lower. Streamers tickled heads and would occasionally fall and attach themselves to passing partygoers. People walked around with new colors in their hair. Glitter and paper hats, the floor a sticky stew of spilled cocktails and confetti. Everything loud and wet and close.

    On stage Funk Def was rocking out. Seven pieces, two horns; they blasted away. The crowd bounced in rhythm, danced and jumped, shoved chairs aside and boogied.

Funk Def featured a blond bombshell up front, shoehorned into a white dress, with swirling boas, a tiara and a pair of glasses that would make Liberace blanch. Teetering on heels, her cleavage was impossible to ignore.

The place was jammers. Two bartenders were trying to hold off the thirsty mob. Drinks were slopped together and shoved out. Registers stuffed, the tip jars overflowed with green cash money.

Down behind the bar, past the walk-in cooler and stacked cases of empty beer bottles and down the poorly lit cement hallway in the office were the cognescenti.

Easy Ed kicked back in the high leather chair, his feet up on the desk. Sitting on the desk facing him was Amy Hawkin, a shorty one year out of Ann Arbor and just named to Winterland Ski Patrol. She had been hooking up with Ed lately. It had been on the down low, until tonight. Wardo, Winterland's only professional (read: merely factory sponsored) skier was busy rolling a spliff. On the couch sat Greg Hamilton and Kent Jennings, who speed rapped about the nefarious dealings of Starbucks coffee. Sliding off two chairs were three drunk chicks; the Tres Hermanas were in the house. Danny was meant to be supervising the bartenders, but was taking a breather in the office. He'd only be in their way out there. He'd been dating Jen #2 lately, and spent most nights at their apartment above the shop.

Ed sipped coffee. He'd been sober now for two months and didn't miss it one bit. The rest of them were drunk and jabbering away when Ed quieted them.

"I'd just like to thank everyone for coming tonight, for all your help getting this place up and running. The first night I opened I had three people come in. I didn't know—"

"He didn't know what was in a gin and tonic!" said Jennings. Everyone laughed.

"It's true. I had no idea if this was gonna work. And now for the first time tonight I think we had a line out front. Thanks everyone. Happy New Year."

Here, here!

Greg Hamilton went next. "I'd like to thank everyone too. It's been a bumpy few years for me now, but it looks like the sale is just about finalized, I should have the funds by the end of the month. Drinks are on me then!" This got a big cheer.

Danny thanked Wardo for teaching him to ski. Wardo thanked Jah for ganja. Jennings, the oldest by decades, was unsentimental, but raised his glass for every toast.

Jen #1 was thankful for steady business at the shop, and the prodigious snow that had dumped so far that year.

Jen #2 said "I'd like to thank Ed for buying me my first drink when I came in here, and making this the most fun place in town. Oh, and for never charging me cover."

"I told Pete to charge you double."

"Yeah, right. And I'd like to thank this little fella right here, for almost getting me killed on about our third date, when he took me to Trenchtown for the first time."

She eased over to Danny and kissed him softly on the mouth. Then louder, turning to the group. "I'll never forget when you dove into that bonfire of *insanities!*"

"I know!" said Beth.

"That was *sick,* brah."

Even Wardo, never looking up from the ongoing spliff project, agreed that he had gone big.

She smiled at Danny, put her arm playfully around his waist. "Tell me again how you wound up here?"

"Well, I saw this film—"

Just then Pete burst in. "It's a real horror show out there. Two minutes to midnight, you guys wanna come join the party?"

"Yeah, let's take it to the streets, come on," said Ed.

Yeah.

"Then we'll come back and fire up that bomber," said Danny.

Yeah!

"Word," said Wardo.

They rushed out to join the party. Muffled through the wall sounds of Auld Lang Syne as they squeezed single file down the hallway with the flickering buzzing light overhead. When they emerged in the humid barroom, the band had just launched an old Prince tune, a brassy version of *1999*. They cognoscenti waded in and were enveloped by the dance party. Big smiles. Cameras flash. As much beer in the air as in the glasses. Orange, blue and yellow stage lights. Everyone dancing. Hugging. Kissing.

Outside, snow continued to fall from the dark Colorado sky. The bar was still packed when the cops arrived.

Part Three
One Bright Morning

Chapter Twelve

Danny woke up in the afternoon, unsure he was alive. He head was throbbing, his hangover acute. Still, it was a powder day.

It dumped all night, and if there was one thing he'd learned, there was no cure for a hangover—no cure for anything—like a bluebird morning. For some meteorological reason that he couldn't comprehend, it mostly snowed here at night. You'd wake up to a blue sky over fluffy white snow. Bluebird.

Jen # 2 lay next to him, the down comforter up to her navel, a pillow over her face. Everyone had the day off. They'd made the decision after the Irish Car Bombs—but before the shots of Grand Marnier—not to open the burrito shop. Trappers was closed too. (Indeed it would take a cleaning crew a full day to get the bar ready to re-open, such had been the chaos.)

Jen stirred next to him. "What time is it?"

"Almost one."

"What day is it?"

"Stay here, I'll get you some juice." No one was up in the apartment. Danny looked out the window at B Street and estimated fifteen inches had fallen. He took a slug of cold OJ from the carton, then filled a glass for Jen.

He set the glass on the nightstand and sat next to her in the bed. He kissed her cheek.

"Will you come skiing with me?"

"I need sleep. I feel like ass. You go."

"You don't mind?"

"I don't mind. Buy me dinner?"

"You got it." He got up and slipped into his base layer.

He puked in a snow bank on Main Street. Twenty minutes later he caught a chair to the summit.

***

Ed didn't get much sleep. Amy had stayed over. They hadn't slept together yet, but she'd been staying over. She was confused, still

91

hung up on a guy in Santa Cruz. Mostly she and Ed just slept with their arms around each other. He looked at her straight dark hair spread on the pillow. She was lovely.

He felt like shit. That visit from the cops had him worried. The smirking, smug, pig faced grins. Something was up.

They'd only stayed at the bar long enough to deliver the message. What the hell did Turcotte want with him? Luckily, no one seemed to notice them. In three minutes they were back outside. The band never even stopped playing.

What a night. It all came back to him. He'd really pulled it off. Not just the night, but the whole thing. He ran the best bar in town. (Granted, the Elks weren't much competition.) But his place was the joint. Pats on the back, hand shakes. Girls had kissed him. Amy didn't mind. Even when a few of them kissed her. It was one big sloppy fun fest. He shuddered to think of the condition they'd left the bar in when they walked out after three. Had he even locked it?

The bar! The bar was going better than he ever imagined. Since he'd hired Danny things were smooth. The guy was a like a piston. He just never stopped. Even on busy nights Ed could leave him alone out there. It was only when Danny had the night off that Ed needed two bartenders.

Hamilton was right, things picked up when the hill opened. Almost every day through the fall new arrivals pulled up in Cherokees and Subarus full of fun junkies. Hippies, trustafarians, dirt bags, ski bums… call em what you want, Ed loved them. They bought liquor like the ship was going down.

You'd see them in town, walking their dogs, hackey-sacking even in the snow. Some had cardboard signs HAVE PLACE TO STAY, NEED WORK. Ed had a stack of applications. He couldn't hire any more people, Danny's roommates had rounded out the staff. But he often let them use the bathroom or offered them water when they stopped by.

When Meg tended bar the place would be packed with drooling guys. Ed had figured out inventory now, even got a little price break from the distributor when his sales crossed a certain point. Ed still hadn't met the landlord. Miller had come up only once, saw that he was doing well, and driven back to Denver the same day.

Jennings had been invaluable. And his columns were hilarious.

Jennings! Better give him a call, maybe he'd know what this meeting was about.

***

Ed couldn't get Jennings on the line, and there was no time to drive up to his place. He was supposed to see Turcotte at two. He showered, threw on a shirt, and drove down to the station on the south side, near the river.

The building was a flat brick affair, tan colored and cheerless. Ed parked next to the Winterland Sheriff Department Blazer and shut off the ignition.

Inside he was forced to wait almost thirty minutes.

"Ed, I'm sorry you had to wait. I've been dealing with some drunks we took in last night. Sorriest sons a bitches you ever saw."

Turcotte sat behind his desk. He had a pit bull face and big shoulders stretched his brown shirt.

"That's all right, Sheriff, I have the day off."

"You might be taking a whole lotta days off."

"How's that?"

"One of my undercovers made a purchase of a Class A substance on your premises last night shortly after one am. This is serious Ed. I need you to tell me right now what you know about this."

"I don't know anything about that, dude." He affected the familiar just to annoy the prick. He smelled bullshit.

"He said it was one of your employees. Now I make one phone call to judge Olsen in Milner and I get a warrant. I want you to tell me, are we gonna find anything in your bar that shouldn't be there?"

"The only thing that shouldn't be there is confetti and some piles of puke. The place was packed last night. But no one's selling any drugs. Dude."

"You watch that smart mouth, son. I could arrest you right now and you'll spend New Year's Day in my holding cell. They tell me it gets mighty cold in there when we forget to turn on the heat. You read me?"

"I read you, and Sheriff, nobody on my staff is selling drugs. If they do, please bust them. Be my guest. I don't want that shit in my place. But I'm telling you, there was no deal in there last night."

"You can guarantee I'll be watching real close from now on. I find out you knew about this, you're looking at a conspiracy to violate charge right there. That's five to ten, mandatory minimum. Now get out of my sight."

***

When Ed got in the car his defiant façade cracked a little. What that fuck was all that? Before he drove away, he noticed that the back, where the holding cells were located, was untouched snow. They hadn't arrested any drunks.

***

Danny slid off the lift and poled a few strokes to the hump that dropped down to White Carpet. He let his momentum carry him over the edge and eased down and around to the left, to the beginner side of the mountain. Where he'd learned.

Wardo had been a regular since Danny started at Trappers, and in exchange for a pretty much open tab, he'd given Danny a pair of his sponsor's skis and showed him the basics. Lean forward, keep your knees bent. He'd been helpful, and Danny's natural athleticism soon took over. He found that the quick footwork that served him so well carving up Big Ten midfields were an asset to skiing as well. He still fell—all the time—but as he learned to control his edges he could handle some steep terrain. Trying to keep up with Wardo, who went downhill like a weight dropped from a building, was the best training imaginable.

Within a few weeks Danny could handle most any terrain on the mountain, and by Christmas he was proficient to bomb even the black diamonds, his low center of gravity and high pace carrying him threw any uncertainty. His style was less artful than Wardo's effortless grace, but full of derring do. He loved going fast. He could see why people got addicted to this.

He noticed no tracks going into Hinterland, always a relief. He skied in through the trees until he lost momentum. There was so much snow he had to unclip and hike it. What had Wardo told him? A five minute hike eliminates ninety-five percent of the skiers. Sometimes a hundred percent. His heart beat faster as he thought about first tracks.

At the top of the lift most everyone turned right to the steeps and bumps and best tree skiing. Only the feeble beginner turned left to ski White Carpet, Rabbit and Honey Do. They lead down the northern flank of the hill, which flattened out like a parking lot near the bottom and then required a traverse and a rope tow to get back to the chairlift. It was a decent place for kids, but since Winterland drew so few families, it was a little used quadrant of the hill.

He'd discovered Hinterland very much by accident. Literally! A near accident in his pants.

He'd ridden the lift with his bladder about to burst, then skied off the lift to the left, turned a hard right and skied a ways into the tightening aspens to take a piss. He was about to squirt when he heard voices from the trail behind him, so, embarrassed, he poled deeper into the woods and relieved himself. And then he saw it.

Through the trees…a broad shoulder of white. He zipped up and skied over. The snow was deep, almost to his chest. The trees grew tight, he'd had to turn sideways to slip between a few of them, then climb over a fifteen foot boulder to get a look. But there it was. The trees abruptly opened to a wide meadow that overlooked a virgin slope just sparkling in the sun. It was so close to the summit that through the trees he could make out the whining of the lift and muted shouts of skiers unloading.

Try White Knuckle!

I'll meet you on Sunset by the cat track!

He couldn't see the bottom, but the run was perfectly pitched. In bounds it would be another blue diamond cruiser, but hundreds of yards wide and without a single track. He'd dropped in that day and ridden down a few dozen turns when he got scared. He had no idea where it lead. So he'd unclipped and hiked back up. Which was a little more aerobic than he'd hoped. He was dumping sweat in the fifteen minutes it took him to get back up. He'd made note of the location and went back to the groomed runs.

He hadn't gone back right away. One bad hangover and then his first night hooking up with Jen #2 had kept him off the hill for a couple of days. When he returned there was still only one track down the face. His track. Incredible.

So for a few weeks it was his private preserve. After a storm, the hill would get skied hard. The groomers were the first to go. The ski patrol had first shot. They went up early to check conditions. Then the lifties would have their fun. It was the only thing that made the job worthwhile. (Certainly the $7.30/hour that Hamilton paid wasn't the attraction). But once they got the maze shoveled out, and the chairs brushed off, they could ski laps for forty-five minutes until the lifts opened to the public.

Then the pass holders and any day ticket buyers were turned loose. On a busy day they'd have the groomers tracked out by noon, and reduced to packed powder by the time the hill closed at four. The trail edges held deeper snow for a few days after a storm, the trees perhaps for a week. You had to search far and wide for snow that lasted longer than a week without at least some tracks.

Of course, you rarely had to wait a week between storms. It often snowed for days on end. Searching for the deep stuff was a shared passion for the partisan junkies and powder stashes were a closely guarded secret.

Danny had gone back to Hinterland almost every day for two weeks. He skied further and further down until he found that the run bottomed out in a valley after perhaps eight hundred feet of vertical. His legs grew used to the effort, and he'd purchased some snow shoes that he kept now in his backpack when he skied. If he was chugging it took him about forty minutes to get back up. Then five to catch his breath. It was grueling, but worth while. The sensation, that floating, grooving, carving, controlled freefall that only steep and deep powder offered. It was exhilarating. It came to dominate his thoughts.

Only after weeks of ripping this powder stash on his own did he push any further along the ridge. It had gotten tracked out. Meaning that his tracks (occasionally) touched each other. So one day he brought some extra water and a granola bar and pushed past the Meadow and through another clump of trees. Here he found some rocks and chutes that were scary, even covered as they were with several feet of fluff. He'd dropped in cautiously, side slipping a ways down to get the feel for it, then found a perfect rock to drop. He'd sidestepped back up a bit, took a deep breath and pointed his tips at it. He lifted off the end of the rock and dropped fifteen feet through space into the bottomless champaign powder. He'd been bathtubbed—landed on his back with his limbs spread, but it was painless. He'd let out a whoopee and hiked back up to do it again and again. After he'd dropped the rock a few times, he skied further down, exploring as he went. It was a steep, rock-lined gully that ended abruptly at some impassable boulders. He called this place Trenchtown.

And so it went for much of late December. He'd usually take a warm up run on the hill proper, always glad to have that chairlift under his ass for the ride back up, then sneak into Hinterland for some steep angled ecstasy. He pushed further and further along the ridge, checking out lines, learning the nuances. It wasn't all skiable. There were some mandatory airs. Some spots you got only fifty feet down before the run cliffed out. He'd had one close call on an exposed rockband that dropped onto a pile of boulders. Some careful sidestepping had gotten him out of that, his heart in his throat the whole time. Other runs were too flat to carry you through the powder, and some were just too short to be worth it.

One day he'd decided to see how far the ridge went. He hiked for almost an hour, often fighting the urge to just drop in. Then he'd rounded a bend and looked up at some familiar fang-like boulders. He was on the back side of Fox Tail Pass, just below where they'd camped in September. It was incredible, all this terrain, so vast it gave him vertigo. And not a single soul seemed to know about it. Occasionally he'd see snowmobile tracks in the valley, but never ski tracks.

Soon he had his favorite spots wired. The initial field he called Mellow Mood. Then there was Trenchtown. A perfectly spaced group of aspens became Hammersmith Palais. A distant powder field he called Do Re Mi. The rock hop was Pretty Boy Floyd.

One day, after weeks of secretive greed, he knew it was big enough—indeed that *he* was big enough—to share.

But who could he tell? Danny knew that he owed Wardo. But he also knew that Wardo had a big mouth. He'd tell Ed, but Ed didn't ski anyway. He occasionally went up with a borrowed snowboard, but it wasn't his bag. His roommates? They were likely to knee cap him for keeping it a secret, but those guys could wait.

So under threat of death and mayhem, he confided in Jen. She was a sick skier, much better than him, in fact. Indeed on early morning groomed corduroy he couldn't stay with her. Her soaring high speed arcs were a sight to behold. But she was getting better in the powder, too, and couldn't get enough of it. She'd learned to ski in Ice Station Vermont and to her, like any boilerplate-skidding New England die hard, the western powder was straight butter.

So he took her out there one day after they got some freshies. And she'd gone mental. Yelping in the pure joy of it. Knowing Mellow Mood as he did, he got down before she did. She skied up, made no effort to stop, and fly-tackled him back into the snow.

"That was fucking rad!"

They were buried, covered in snow, tangled in skis, their hair slick, their faces wet with sweat and snow and kissing, giggling like fools.

That night she cooked him eggplant parmesan and they made love in her big bed while candles burned.

Chapter Thirteen

That afternoon Danny skied for a while, and it was deep as shit, but his legs weren't there and he quit early. He hiked up, peeked out of the trees, saw that no one was looking, then doubled back to the lift and dropped in to the right, down Lightning. He made some looping giant slalom turns, taking it easy, and was soon at the base area.

He got back to the shop, walked up the narrow steps to the apartment and found the girls in full recovery mode. Around the living room they lounged in pajamas and furry slippers, surrounded by Gatorades, coffees, waters, juice.

"How you guys doin' in here?"

"I'm never-drinking-again."

"Yeah, can you please ban me from your bar? That place is bad for my health."

"Well, *someone* kept ordering those shots of Jaeger."

"Don't even say it."

"Deep breaths, girls," advised Jen #1. Next to her on the couch, Beth was either asleep or dead.

"How was it Danny? Did you go to…ahh…"

"Yeah, deep as shit, but I was too tired," said Danny.

It hadn't snowed in like four days. "What was deep as shit?" asked Jen #1.

Danny and his Jen exchanged a look. Her eyes pleaded. "They're my best girls."

"All right."

"Yay! You tell them, it's your place."

"What's your place?" said Jen #1. Even Beth opened her eyes, semi-alive.

"Well, seeing as how you ladies have been kind enough to let me crash here so often, I guess it's only fair that you be among the first to know. I found a pretty good stash. Better than pretty good. You might say it's in-fucking-sane."

"It's wild girls, wait til you see it. He took me there last week."

"It's sick. I'll take you there tomorrow. But you can't tell anyone."

"Ooh!"

"Is this the field between Straight Shot and Ramrod?"

"It makes that look like a postage stamp."

"My, how exciting."

Danny hopped in the shower and had just drenched his hair when Jen #2 came in.

"Danny, Ed's on the phone."

"Tell him I'll call him back."

"He said it's urgent."

Danny, dripping in a towel, padded out to the living room. Cat calls from the girls. "Woo woo!"

"Yo."

"Dude, we have a problem."

"What's up?"

"I don't know exactly. Can you come over?"

"Give me ten minutes."

***

"What's up?" asked Danny. They were standing in Ed's kitchen.

"Remember when those deputy sheriffs stopped by last night?"

"...Vaguely."

"I had to go see Turcotte this morning. And he accused me of selling drugs. At the bar. I think he's full of shit. But did you see anything go down last night?"

"Well, I mean, besides like Wardo's joint?"

"No, he said it was Class A. Meaning like coke or smack. You didn't see anyone, did you?"

"Just drunk, far as I know. I didn't see anything like that."

"I was around that stuff when I was in college, I can usually tell when someone's glued up. But I spent most of the night in the office."

"Well, I guess anything is possible. We must have had two hundred people in there."

"Yeah, I know he's full of shit. He told me he had a cell full of drunks, and his holding tank hadn't been opened since it snowed. And he said the deal, which, oh yeah, he said took place between one of his "undercovers" so called, and one of our staff—took place at one am. And the deputies stopped by right after midnight. Something is funny here."

"Well, if he said it was someone who worked there, we know that's not true. It was just me and my roommates last night. And none of those guys do blow, never mind sell it. I'd know."

100

"Yeah, I know. But he's definitely coming after us. So just keep your eyes open. I've got to talk to Jennings, maybe be knows what's up."

"Good idea.."

"It's just fucking weird, man."

***

After Danny left Ed tried Jennings at the Wire, but they said he'd hadn't been in all day. Ed tried to think.

There was no *way* Turcotte knew about the Miami thing, right? It was a one-time cash deal with people he'd never met and would never see again. Even Sponge hadn't known the guy's name. That was out.

Hammer? He was a prick, but no way he held sway over the sheriff. Jennings made it sound like he didn't have a pot to piss in. He sold blow, Ed was pretty sure, but he hadn't set foot in the bar since being axed. And Turcotte would know him anyway, and know that he didn't work for Ed. That was out.

So what was it? Maybe someone did sell something, but the timing inconsistency…the other weird lies about the prisoners? Something was wrong. He was brooding when Amy got home from her patrol shift.

"How was it, babe?"

"Not bad. Aside from some hangovers, everyone was just psyched to ski powder. What's with you?"

"I had a run in with the Sheriff this morning."

"What did he want?"

"I have no idea."

***

Danny stopped by the green and white house and checked in with the roomies. They were recovering too, none had gone up on the hill. He asked them about the alleged deal, and they doubted it too.

"Yeah, and I was helping a dude who'd passed out in the bathroom. Right around one, actually. Nothing went down in there. I was there," said Brian.

"Oh yeah! That guy was shit housed," said Kev.

"I finally poured him into a cab, stuffed a ten in his shirt pocket. Hopefully he's still alive."

"But you guys didn't see anyone selling yay-yo?"

"Naw."

"Nothing like that."

101

"No dude."

"I didn't think so. But still, we're gonna have to be careful in there now, they're watching us."

***

Danny took Jen #2 to Santarpio's for a late supper. They'd finally been hungry once their stomachs settled. They shared vegetable lasagna, salad and some garlic bread. Water, no wine. They were in bed before ten.

"So you want to take the girls to Mellow Mood tomorrow, Jen?"

"As long as you don't mind sharing."

"No, they're great. How many burritos have they given me?"

***

It was all going according to plan for Nut Richards. Degbert had crafted a honey of a deal. One-point-four-one and no more. They were just waiting on Hamilton's signature on the purchase and sales agreement. And now they had their eyes on some other parcels in town. Nut really wanted to make his mark. Remake the town in his own image. The more he thought about having his own playground, the more he liked it. So he'd steadily been divesting himself of assets, selling off drilling rights here, platform leases there, and building a war chest. If he could divide and conquer, keep these yokels from knowing his intentions, he could buy a lot of them out before they knew what hit them. The ski area was the tip of the iceberg.

***

Two nights later, Ed opened the bar around seven. It was dead. It was only medium busy by eleven, most people were exhausted from skiing powder for three straight days. Ed was in the office, about to call Amy, when Jennings stumbled in. He was shit cocked.

"You drinking cough syrup again?"

"Ed my son, I dance with angels."

"Where have you been? I called the Wire looking for you."

"I've been out of work since I sustained a terrible injury in a hunting accident."

"Oh, man. What were you hunting?"

"Poontang."

"Nice. Get you a drink?"

"Already taken care of." He produced a silver flask from inside his sheep shearer vest.

"Let me ask you something, Kent. What's the story with Turcotte?"

"Well, see the problem with Turcotte is not that he's got much power, it's that he knows it can't be taken away from him. He's got the ranching and church vote, what's left of em anyway, and that's all he needs. He runs from a district with slightly more bi-partisan support than the last re-election campaign of Idi Amin. He's dug in. Why, did he give you a parking ticket?"

"No, he accused me of selling coke. Well, some Class A substance, anyway."

"He's just trying to rattle your cage. He knows this is the bottom feeder bar."

"You can't talk about my loyal clientele in such libelous terms."

"It's only libel if you print it, if you say it its slander. Believe me, I've been sued for both." They laughed. "No, he's probably just scared. Town is changing. The ranching days are fading. As you can see, there's a new breed coming in. Skiers, young people. He sees hippy and he thinks drug addict. It's got to be driving him nuts."

"It's just odd. I asked everyone who was here last night, no one saw anything, plus I caught him in at least one other lie in the five minutes I spent with him."

"You know how to tell if Turcotte is lying?"

"How?"

"His mouth moves. That's an old one."

"I think it's true, though. He's full of shit."

"You're wise my son. Let me ask around, see if I can figure out why he's busting your ball sack."

"Thanks man."

***

Word was out around town. Greg Hamilton was gonna cash in. There was some big developer who was gonna buy the mountain and remake it into another Vail. And people were excited. For the long-suffering locals, it was a chance to get a return on their investments, or at least cash out and move on. And the ski crowd weren't totally against it, they just wanted to rip powder. If the new guy was gonna modernize the lifts and build some restaurants, hey, all the better.

So all around, businesses started to gussy themselves up for a potential sale. People got ready, there was a train coming.

With the sale all but guaranteed, Hamilton was able to obtain some bridge financing from the bank, which fronted him fifty-thousand dollars against profits from the sale. He immediately threw an all company party in the lodge, complete with shrimp and steak and kegs of beer. In the next week's payroll there were tenure based bonuses. Even first year lifties got a few hundred bucks cash stuffed in their pay packets.

Hamilton felt good to be able to reward the hardworking people who had helped him open this year, when all they were guaranteed was a few bucks an hour and a ski pass that might be worthless when the mountain crashed into bankruptcy court.

Jennings came out with an editorial warning about the new mystery owner, refreshing people's memory to the real estate investment trust that seemed like a white knight to the cattle yard, only to be a rat in shit-stained clothing, sent I.O.U. But it did little to stem the tide. Real estate fever began to sweep through town.

* * *

The next day Jen #2 drew the short straw. So while she got Tres Hermanas ready to open, Jen #1 and Beth met Danny at the base area. With him were Meg, Kev and Brian. Pete was too hung over to move.

All were sworn to secrecy and tingling with excitement.

As they approached Hinterland, Danny noticed a new track leading into the woods at the turnoff. The fat, single track of a snowboard. Luckily it dead-ended forty feet in front of some yellow snow. Secret safe.

They skied a few laps on Mellow Mood, then continued on to Trenchtown. They were going crazy, rooster tails flying off the back of Brian's snowboard, Kev's lanky frame angled deep into turns, Beth almost landed a 360 off Pretty Boy Floyd. By two they were all exhausted and skied back down the front, into town. They stopped by Tres for some chips with guacamole and an iced tea. Their conversation was muted with awe. The wide open looks on their faces told the story of wonder. Holy shit.

Danny left to get ready for his bar shift.

He opened Trappers four days a week now, usually between six and seven. It was rarely busy before ten, but he got the limes cut and the ice loaded and the bottles stacked. There was a band that night, so he'd have to get them checked into their hotel and be around for sound check. When he arrived he found the door boarded shut with screaming orange stickers taped to the windows.

CLOSED PER ORDER OF
WINTERLAND SHERIFF'S DEPARTMENT

He ran the three blocks to Ed's place.

Chapter Fourteen

"Miller, it's Ed."

"What's happening, my man?"

"I'll tell you what's happening. I got shut down today. They blocked the fucking door. I can't even get in there to get my stuff."

"What are you talking about? Who blocked it?"

"Turcotte."

"Who?"

"The fucking sheriff. He got me shut down pending some bogus narcotics investigation. He's got some trumped up charge that someone was selling drugs out of the bar."

"Was it Hammer?"

"I fired Hammer."

"Smart move. Shit man, I don't know what to tell you."

"You never had a problem with Turcotte?"

"I never even heard of him. You paid the rent, right? That's the only thing I can think, like it's an eviction or something. I mean, taxes wouldn't even be due yet, it's not that."

"Yeah, I've been sending checks to the PO Box you gave me, and they've been getting cashed. I don't have a clue what's going on."

"If you can, talk to the landlord. I never met him either, keeps to himself, but I know he owns most of that block."

***

Ed jumped in his truck and drove up to Jennings's place above town. He wound down the flag-lined driveway, past the full sized grizzly bear sculpture and parked by the row of psychedelic painted toilets.

He found Jennings inside, brewing beer.

"Sorry to barge in, man, I've got a major situation here."

"Turcotte?"

"You got it. As we speak I'm locked out of my own bar."

"Shit, I was afraid of this."

"Did you hear something?"

"Sort of. Sit down."

"OK, about two weeks ago your amigo Jack Ass got busted. Routine traffic stop, but Hammer's all glued up, can't shut his fucking mouth, and they get suspicious. They toss the car and Hammer's sitting on fifteen little baggies of Columbian party powder. They bust him, and he tells them he bought it at Trappers."

"Bullshit."

"It is bullshit, even Turcotte knows that. But there's where it gets interesting."

***

Danny and Jen #2 dropped by Kev's around dinner time. Pete was stirring a big pot of chili. Danny relayed the bad news. Pete pulled a tray of hot cornbread out of the oven and they all settled around the table to eat.

"Well, this sucks," said Kev.

"Yeah, we're pretty much all unemployed at this point. Ed thinks he can get the bar open again in a few days. But maybe not, too. He's gonna need a lawyer, it's gonna get expensive. This is a mess," said Danny.

They finished their chili and flopped in the living room.

"All right, let's say he can't get the bar open?"

"Well, we start looking for work," said Kev.

"Ahh! My least favorite word," said Pete.

"Yeah, good luck. Everything in town is taken. Haven't you seen the dudes panhandling on Main Street?" said Brian.

"Is there another bar we could work at?" asked Meg.

"Yeah, *you* could probably get hired anywhere you go. Us ugly mugs aren't gonna be so lucky," said Pete.

"There's only one other bar, at the Elks club. I went in there once to piss. Yipes. I would describe it as like a room full of angry lumberjacks meets a Klan meeting, then add whiskey. I wouldn't go back in there without an Uzi," said Danny.

"Were there any chicks?" They laughed.

"Well, we all bought passes, and the mountain is still open. I would think the new owner would have to honor the existing passes. So we can still ski out the season," said Brian.

"And we've paid the rent through April, so we at least have a place to stay. It could be worse," said Kev.

"Yeah, I asked Ed. He said the only other liquor license in town is owned by the hill, but Hamilton hasn't even had the money to stock the bar in two years, so its just sitting there. Maybe, I mean, worst case scenario, Ed could work something out with him," said Danny.

"Turcotte here."

"Did you talk to our friend?"

"Did more than talk. I got his ass locked out on the street. I'm sure we have his attention now. Don't you worry, I'm on it."

"Nice work."

***

"So the worst kept secret in town is that Winterland is in play. We've been running a story a week about it, at least. So now the whole town has their britches in a knot, trying to cash in."

"What does this have to do with my place? I don't want to sell."

"Yeah, but your landlord does. Name's Klein. Helmut Klein. He's one of these respectable kraut burghers. Owns half of Main Street. So my sources tell me that the buyer is this tycoon who calls himself "Nut" Richards, if you can believe that. This Richards prick wants to buy the hill, then buy the rest of town to go with it. Turn it into some kind of cowboy theme park or some damn shit. Made his name in Texas using his little oil company to go after bigger oil companies. Took over Nerper Oil and turned their pension fund into his own piggy bank. He's a greedy fucker and he's got deep pockets. So Klein, who's holding all these dead leases, he sees this as his lottery ticket. He offers to sell out lock stock and barrel. But Richards is smart, he doesn't want to deal with any stragglers, he's only buying distressed properties. Wants to buy everything up cheap and real quiet, like. Ironically, since your place is starting to turn around, it's worth less to them. Richards wants a clean slate. Klein can't sell it until he can get rid of you."

"I've got a lease for the next twenty-one months. He can't kick me out if I pay the rent."

"Of course, you are correct. But Klein can put heat on you. And guess who was the biggest contributor to Turcotte's re-election campaign? Bingo. I'm sure he's promised our good sheriff a nice little kickback if he can hasten your exit any."

***

Danny and Jen #2 walked home around ten. For the first time in days it wasn't snowing. Danny looked up at the stars and held her hand tight. The bar looked like it was fucked. He felt bad for the roommates, he'd gotten them all jobs there. He himself had less than two hundred bucks left. He'd been living on bar tips.

"You know, you can work at the burrito shop if you want."

"Ok, I hadn't really thought about that. Well, yeah. Thanks."

"Obviously you're a hard worker. And the girls love you. I don't think it hurt your standing any that you showed them your stash."

"Yeah, that never hurts. Say, what's your company's policy on dating employees?"

"Come upstairs. I think this particular policy is better demonstrated than explained."

***

Ed tried to go fishing the next morning, but he was too pissed. He tried a few casts before packing it in and getting back in the car. He wasn't gonna sit still while they fucked with his business.

***

"Who let you in here?"

"Are you Klein?"

"Yes."

"I own Trappers and I'd like to know why you're trying to evict me?"

"Why don't you have a seat?"

Ed sat down. The guy was gray and stooped, but this didn't temper Ed's rage.

"What's this all about?"

"Business. I'm sure you understand."

"I understand that I've got a successful business and you're trying to fuck with it."

"There is no need for this coarse language, my son. I will tell you what I have to say. And then you will understand. My grandfather came to this country from the Sudenten, in Germany. This, for an American, is like being from Alabama. From nowhere. He worked hard, built himself into something. He started with one truck in Cincinnati."

"Look, save me the Ellis Island tearjerker."

"I am an old man. My family is gone. This is all I have left. And I wish to live out my days in the sun. I am selling this property, and I'm afraid there's nothing you can do about that."

108

"I can still pay my rent on time, I have a lease with your signature on it, in case you forgot, and that's good for almost another two years."

"This is true."

"So right there I'm off the hook. And what is the deal with siccing Turcotte on me?"

"You think I control the sheriff? You give me too much credit."

"Well, no one's selling drugs down there, and I'm staying put. I'm sorry if you don't like it."

"I don't know anything about drugs. You rely on the strength of this contract. Which you have signed. Which I have signed. You have been raised to have faith in the system. And this is good. And if you have read the lease carefully you know that any change of ownership ends the contract. When I sell the building, our lease contract is null and void, as it would be on any change of ownership. I'm sorry Mr. Miller."

"Miller? I'm not Miller, I'm Ed Stallings." And as soon as he said it, he knew he was fucked. *Any change in ownership.*

A quick glint in the old German's eye. Then it was gone. "Then it appears the lease has already been voided. A concern called the Galveston & and Colorado Ski Partners LLC is to be the new ownership group. They will own the building in which your bar operates. If your lease is to be renewed, it is up to them and beyond my control. Good day, Mr. Stallings."

***

Danny and Jen #2 lay in bed. Danny wanted to be fresh for his first day of work in the exciting world of hand rolled foods, but this bar deal was gnawing at him.

"I just feel bad for Ed. He's such a great guy. He really loved that bar, loved the way people came in to see him. He was telling me he used to party pretty hard, and now he's stopped all that. Like his life was turning around. I feel terrible. I hope he doesn't start drinking."

"I know. There's got to be something we can do for him, Danny. Half the town was hanging out there, now where will they go?"

"I don't know. It just sucks all the way around."

"Well, maybe you could show him our stash?"

"Who's stash?"

"Danny's stash. Dan the Man, I forgot."

"No, you're right. That would cheer him up some. Then again he's not that into skiing, or snowboarding. Mostly he talks about fishing. The thing with Hinterland is…" He sat up in bed.

"The thing is what?"

"We'll tell Hamilton about Hinterland!"

"What good will that do? He's only gonna own the place for another few weeks."

"Yeah, but I get the feeling he doesn't want to sell."

"Yeah, right, you ever hear him talk about the place? He can't wait to sell. He pretty much has to or he's going bankrupt."

Danny got up, pacing now. "Yeah, but if all of a sudden the size of the ski area doubled, or tripled, maybe it would be more profitable. He could stay in business."

"There's no lifts back there. Not everyone is gonna wanna hike all day."

"Yeah…so he makes it, yeah, he makes it like ski cat terrain. He gets a ski cat, and we shuttle people in that. Oh man, for all that powder, he could clean up, people would pay good money. Usually, powder cat skiing is like two or three hundred bucks a day. He gets a cat back there, people ski down, they bring em right back up. You get lift serviced backcountry terrain. Best of both worlds."

There was a pause.

"That's good Danny. That could really work."

"It would totally work, its huge back there, you haven't seen the half of it. We get a bunch of cats, running laps, increase the ticket prices, maybe, just a little, they'd still be a deal and for what you'd…I gotta talk to Hamilton."

Chapter Fifteen

By St. Patrick's Day the pressure on Hamilton was unbearable. His lawyer had used every quasi-legal stalling technique known to man. The deal was teed up and ready to go, and Richards was chomping at the bit. He didn't know how much longer he could legally hold the guy off, seeing as how they had a signed purchase and sales agreement in place. Hamilton was on the hook, because he had to sell to the highest bidder, and there was only one interested party. Even his creative lawyer couldn't get him out of that.

Greg loved the idea of Hinterlands. Since Danny had taken him out there in January it burned his consciousness. He'd fast tracked a lease obligation with the Forest Service, who controlled the land. They were happy to give him a provisional 99 year lease for most of the terrain that Hinterland covered (like government lackeys anywhere, they loved anything that generated revenue) it was just that no matter the level of arm twisting, legal wrangling and flat out begging that he employed, the application could only be nudged along so quickly. Hamilton had burned through his bridge financing and most of his cash reserves to speed it along as fast as he could, now it was just a matter of time. He had to close by April first, and he still hadn't heard from the feds.

It was a great idea. He'd skied enough crowded, tracked out powder in his life, waited in enough lift lines, seen enough crowded slopes to know that the wide open terrain back there was a bonanza. He couldn't make money with the ski area per se, but if he could get a powder cat skiing operation working, he knew he'd draw from the reserves of hard cores willing to pay top dollar for untracked powder. But he had less than two weeks to find out if he got the lease. He was running out of time.

He was making money again. He'd hired Ed as entertainment director, with plans on refurbishing the sagging bar and grill and having Ed run it like Trappers. But so far they'd been unable to resurrect the liquor license, currently held up by the town council appeals board.

***

Ed had mostly adjusted to his new life. He missed Trappers. He'd finally been able to go and get his personal effects out, under supervision of two smirking deputies. Miller had even offered to refund some of Ed's purchase price, but he'd declined. He washed his hands of the whole matter. All he had left was the revenue from the few weeks that the bar had been open. The cash from the deal in Miami was gone, sunk into a bar that was never coming back.

It had taken Ed a while to bounce back. Many times he'd been tempted to dive into a bottle and ride out the winter that way. But he held off. Ironically, it was Jennings, a man who drank like a minky whale, who helped to keep him sober. Giving him pep talks, taking him fishing. He went fishing almost every day. And he'd started to get proficient.

He had a secret spot of his own now. Past the railroad bridge there was an oxbow as the Arapahoe turned south. As the river wrapped around a massive boulder, there was a sweet spot in the still water behind, accessible by a treacherous wade across slick rocks. But there was a sweet, flat spot to cast from and unless the wind was howling from the south, it was available almost every day. He'd begun to experiment with different flies, varying his retrieve, and finally started to bag fish. Mostly rainbows at first, around three pounds, and some brown trout. Jennings had made it sound like these were mere pikers compared to the cutthroat that would course through in the spring. He was content to fish most mornings before going up on the hill.

He was snowboarding more than ever. He wasn't very good, but came to love the smooth, slicing turns through the soft snow. And on powder morning, surfing that twelve hundred foot wave, he got to love that too.

Amy had moved in. She had gotten him through a lot. She'd finally called hell dude in Santa Cruz and told him that, after five years, it was really over. She was a stable influence on him now, too.

He just missed it. Having the bar, being the man. It was such a waste, Trappers sitting empty while hundreds of thirsty skiers went unslaked. There had been some entreaties, some scouting missions, into the black depths of the Elks. A few people even said it was not horrible.

There were enough people in town now to form a pretty decent party scene, albeit one without center. In lieu of a bar to hang at, the house parties filled the gap.

Still, the bar…What a fucking shame!

He thought back…the first day he opened…hiring Danny…that pig roast! My God, that had been fun. The roaring fire, the pallets burning, then the skis. So much fun. Those powder prayers seemed to have been answered. By March they had already gotten three-hundred-ninety-one inches of snow, and the hill would be open for another six weeks. He missed the bar, but things weren't so bad for Ed these days. He'd become almost a folk hero around town. Everywhere he went people were glad handing him, wishing him well, asking what he was up to next. They all knew he'd been fucked over.

After being depressed for a few weeks, he had an idea. He convinced Hamilton to let him sell beer on the mountain. So he'd rounded up some scrap lumber and he and Danny had built a simple plywood bar by the lower edge of Shoo Fly at the edge of the parking lot. The definition of no-tech, DIY building. A keg was buried in the snow and pumped by foot. There were mismatched chairs and hay bales to sit on. Beer was a buck a cup. Skiers would stop by, grab a brew and head back up the lift. Then after the lift closed, it became the de facto après ski spot. Jennings had an old Airstream trailer on his property, and let Ed haul it down to the parking lot. Ed used this as a home base and set up a blender inside. So now he sold frozen margaritas for three bucks, beers for a buck.

And Ed didn't mind. He lost the bar, lost all his money, but he was doing something that he liked. It was clean and honest, and most everyone in town liked him.

***

Hammer was right about one thing, he did end up owning Trappers. Sort of. At least that's what he told anyone who would listen. He had big plans. Unable to resist even a little rental revenue, Klein had let him rent the space for a few one off events that JackHAMMER! PRODUCTIONS! was promoting. No one showed up. Most everyone in town knew that Ed had been fucked over and stayed away out of loyalty to him. The few stragglers that did stop by were Elks regulars or high school kids looking for drugs. Hammer barely got the doors open.

The first event of his comeback, the Snow Ball Dance (which he considered the height of witty double entendre [although he could define none of these terms]) had been a disaster of Lusitanian proportion. He couldn't get the water turned back on in time, and had to hastily rent a few porta-johns for out back. The event was a fiasco, the band got in a fight on stage, one guy was bottled in the eye (and then sued). Indeed, the conditions in the porta-johns were so abhorrent that criminal charges were later brought. The rest of Hammer's event schedule collapsed when Klein pulled the plug, then the board of health piled on with a five-thousand dollar fine. Under indictment, the production office permanently closed its doors.

As the days ticked down to the sale of Winterland, and the subsequent cashing out by Klein and a dozen other merchants in town, Trappers faded from memory. Vandals stole the sign right off the front of the building and it just became another empty storefront on Main Street. After Hammer's Waterloo the place went back out of business, this time for good.

***

"Wake up, bitches!" Jen #2 was ready to go. Goggles on head, blond braids out the back, down vest over turtle neck, she looked great. Danny buckled his ski boots and the girls got ready for a day on the hill.

They checked in with Kev and Meg in the shop. Everything was stocked up, they were set and waived to their friends as they headed for the slopes. Tres Hermanas was having a banner year. Kev and Meg rotated out every other day with the three girls and Danny. So they could all get some time on the hill before it closed for the season, or was sold, or who knows what?

They went back to Hinterland. There were some tracks, people knew about it now. Word spread fast in a small town. But still, not that many people were willing to hike up through deep snow for twenty minutes only to ride down in two. It took a certain breed.

They took a few laps on Meadow.

"Let's hit the shrine," said Jen #1.

"Word."

They hiked out of the trees by White Carpet. This drew curious looks from two dudes on tele skis just sliding off the lift.

Danny shrugged his shoulders. "Big powder field over here, bro. Just be careful, patrol doesn't sweep back there."

The long hairs looked at each other. "Thanks man!"

Danny and the Tres Hermanas hiked over the hump, then clicked into the their skis and dropped down Bullet. Danny was nearly as good as Jen now. He was half a turn behind her as they sped down Bullet, making GS turns through the packed powder. The sun shone brilliantly overhead. As much as Danny had loved the winter dumps, spring skiing in the magnificent Rockies was even better. It lifted his soul. Making turns in what the locals called hero snow was great. Whereas in the winter you would just float through ghostly light and fluffy powder, in the spring the snow warmed up. So instead of gliding over wispy frozen smoke, now it

114

was more like laying trenches when you sunk your edges into the deep and forgiving damp snow. You could go so fast it was exhilarating, and if you got in trouble, you could just dig your skis in and carve to control velocity.

They were mach-ing, flying top speed down the steep groomed run on Bullet. They were almost at the hidden turnoff. Jen #2 caught an edge, wobbled slightly and regained balance. It was all the opening Danny needed, he dug his right ski in deep, let the parabolic shaped ski do its work, and shot out to the right, a leg bending, low angle, downhill-leg-straight, hand on the snow, trench-digging, high speed g-force turn which shot him off the lip of the trail and into the trees. He caught air—

Woooff!

—he landed in the deep snow in the trees. He kept his momentum. He leaned back and let his tips float. He picked a clean line through the pines and only occasionally crossed another track. Further in he used a few aspens for slalom gates, got some speed, then cut across the hill at a narrow angle, the snow brushing past his shins. He could hear the girls yelping behind him as they danced in rhythm through the aspens. Spraying trees with snow wash. Sun and shadows fell across the fluffy wet mounds of snow between aspens. The route was familiar, the destination euphoric.

Danny let his momentum carry him up onto Rock Steady. He came to a momentary apex before gravity pulled him back down, his tips pointed almost at the sky, stalled it, his skis bending, then at the last second, jump-turned back down the face and came to a stop. And cute maneuver for a guy who hadn't skied five months ago.

The girls skied up behind him moments later. They were snowy and smiling. They clicked out of their skis and went around to the downhill side of the Rock Steady, where a little shrine had been assembled.

Though Pete alone liked to claim credit for it, they had come to the group decision during a drunken late night/early morning. Heading back into town to toke up wasted valuable time on the hill, especially on powder days. Meanwhile, patrol took a wary eye towards mid-trail bong sessions, se they needed a compromise.

So over the course of dozens of clandestine tree runs, this little scene had developed. On the downhill side of Rock Steady there was a little shrine. They started with a framed photo of Bob Marley with his dreads flying wild in a lock whip, his signature Les Paul in hand, his green, red and gold tank top hugging his muscular torso, eyes closed, his right arm extended. That image, nailed to a tree, was the beginning. From here it had spread. And the cool thing was, they only started this place, they did very little of the ultimate decoration. People brought this and that. Soon it was a semi-enclosed den, mostly protected from the wind and snow, and decorated with mardi gras beads and wind chimes, a painting of Jerry Garcia, some Tibetan prayer flags. Some candles jammed into wine bottles served as lights. A Jamaican flag strung between two trees was one wall. An old rug—and they had to hand it to the ambitious pot head who struggled that sucker up here—served as the floor and kept your ass relatively dry. Beth produced a pipe from her jacket's inner pocket and packed a fresh bowl. Danny hit play on the big LL Cool J-style 1980's boom box that someone had left, but the batteries were dead.

Just as well. He had three pretty girls to talk to. They took pulls and passed. Relaxing comfort drifted through them. Danny stuck his skis into the snow and used them for a backrest. Jen # 2 came over and leaned against him. They stared off into the trees. In the distance you could see a corner of town. It was quiet, the only sounds the muffled thumps of snow falling from loaded branches. They could barely hear the yells and calls from the groomers, less than a couple hundred yards away. But miles away.

"Do you think anyone will show up for our party?"

***

Degbert spent the afternoon at the HumVee dealership. He knew the deal would make him the star of Richards Oil, and he'd already been promised a bonus approaching six figures once the it closed. After that the real fun would begin, carving up this shit splat town for fun and profit. It was so close.

***

Jennings woke up in a bush. What the hell? He must have been on his way to work, but didn't make it. Luckily it wasn't too cold out.

It was Wednesday afternoon. He only had about three hours before deadline for his Live Wire column. And he had plenty to write about. He's spent most of the winter railing against Richards's takeover bid, which had become his bete noir. The old guard considered Jennings a burned out relic. But the young people in town started to see him as a drunken mystic. He spouted Baudelaire, he told them about Thomas Wolfe. In his column he evoked words of protest from Woody Guthrie, Joe Strummer, Che Guevara.

116

His tireless ranting had launched a groundswell. He'd been in town long enough to recognize the parallels between this deal and what happened to the cattle yard. He warned everyone who would listen about the white wash of corporate promises and the dangers of monoculture, of too much power in too few hands. Around town now you started to see evidence of a growing resistance movement. On bumpers and snowboards and lift towers there were stickers that said SAVE WINTERLAND and DON'T TEXA$ COLORADO.

Jennings had even started taking collections for a Winterland defense fund.

***

After a few minutes…after nine days…(after a bit, anyway) they got up and wiggled around to get the circulation going again. They clicked into their skis and dropped away from the music shrine and back towards the groomers. Danny sang as he made hopping turns through the snow.

They caught the lift up and took a blissed out run, then another. The sky was clear and the snow was soft. They called to friends from the chair, grouped up, skied in packs that formed and disbanded, drifting around the hill, down Bullet, over the cat track, down Sunshine, over to Ram Rod. Soon the sun was dipping in the western sky and they called it a day. They took one high speed burn down the face, cut across the cat track to Shoo Fly and slid to a stop at Ed's little portable outdoor bar around three-thirty.

Danny did a little 180 hop onto a hay bale and 180 off the other side.

"You're such a dork," teased Jen #2.

"Is that any way to speak to your restaurant manager?"

"We've told you hundreds of times, you are not the manager," said Jen #1.

"If anything, you're on probation for that little situation on Monday," said Beth.

"Yeah, what did you think went in a chicken-pesto again, there, bleach?"

"It was arsenic," said Jen #2.

Danny looked at Ed for backup. "All I did was accidentally put mayo in one burrito. Suddenly I'm like Caligula in the kitchen."

"I'd have fired you for less," said Ed.

"That's it, you tell him Ed," said Jen #1.

"Unbelievable. Can I get a round of brew for these uppity bitches?"

117

"Coming up." Ed pumped the keg with his foot, then filled four cups with icy lager. "On the house."

"Thanks bro." Danny threw five bucks in the tip bucket.

They flopped on hay bales and unbuckled their boots. Jen #1 took hers off completely and rubbed her stocking feet. "Best part of the day, right there."

Danny drained half his beer in one gulp and exhaled, blowing foam from his upper lip. He was feeling good. There were a few dozen people standing around, sipping beers, talking of runs, comparing wipeouts.

"He got *stacked* coming off the cat track."

"We were on Bullet, staightlining, when Durban caught an edge."

"Did you see the touron hosting the yard sale on Honey Do?"

Danny raised and eyebrow at Jen #2. She told him a yard sale was when someone wiped out hard and all their gear went flying. Danny had seen this, some hapless skier prostrate on the hill, double ejected from his skis, goggles over here, gloves over there. Yard sale. He chuckled. It had happened to him.

Laughter and smiles, raccoon tans on goggle-protected faces. Ponytails and high five slaps muted through gloved hands. Beers bought and drained, fun in the sun. From the Airstream Ed had a Widespread bootleg pumping from speakers duct-taped to 2x4's stuck in the snow. More people skied up as the hill emptied and the lifts closed for the day. Ed was filling beers as fast as he could, three or four cups flayed in his fingers, the tap left open.

"Ed! Turcotte!"

Ed swung around to see the loathsome Blazer idling through the clogged lot. The gravel surface was littered with cars. They'd strategically left a Subaru beater between the entrance and the Airstream, for just this type of contingency. Turcotte was forced to stop and get out. In the time it took him to cross the lot, Ed had kicked snow over the tap, burying it. Meanwhile Pete and Brian hauled the blender and handles of Cuervo back inside the Airstream and locked the door. They cut the music just as Turcotte sauntered into the little party.

"Happy St. Patrick's Day, Sheriff."

"Well, well. Stallings. I'll bust your ass so fast it'll make your head spin."

"Bust me for what?"

"Selling alcohol without a liquor license."

"Selling alcohol? I'm not *selling* anything."

"Then what's that bucket of money for?"

118

"We're raising money for the legless."

"Watch it boy." Turning to the Airstream. "So, the booze is hidden in there, right? You think I was born yesterday?" He started to beat on the door. "Open up, Winterland Sheriff's Department!"

Falsetto from within "who ees eet?"

"You heard me, give me that booze, hippy!"

"Come back later. We get sleepy here. Siesta time. Sor-reeee!" Everyone laughed. Someone from the hay bales made pig noises.

"Sorry, dude. No one's selling any al-kee-hol here. These people are just having a beer on the trail of Winterland Ski Area, which is private property."

"Not for long asshole. Everyone knows there's a new owner coming to town. From what I hear he can't wait to hose down your little hobo camp and clean house. I say bring it on." He smashed his nightstick along the bar, spilling a bunch of beers. "Your days are numbered here Stallings. You and the rest of the Woodstock generation. Have a nice day."

He was almost back to the Blazer when he heard "get fucked!" Turcotte stopped and stiffened, but kept walking. He was gonna get that smart ass.

***

After a few nervous minutes the party resumed. After a few more pops Jen #1 said "you guys ready to hit it?"

"Yeah, we need to get set up" said Beth. Jen #2 jumped on a hay bale and shouted "Hey, everyone! Party tonight above Tres Hermanas! Green beer and corned beef and cabbage."

When they got home they put a pot on downstairs and skinned some potatoes and carrots. They dumped the brisket in with the veggies and boiled it beyond recognition, Irish style.

They took turns showering and decorating and by eight the place looked great. They had two kegs of Fat Tire, a powerful green punch, piles of brownies labeled Leaded and Unleaded and several handles of booze with mixers, cups, ice and napkins. Everything was set. They served the food at eight-thirty. No one was there. Jen #2 said "I hope some people stop by."

Too quiet. It was still just them at quarter to nine.

By eleven o'clock the place looked like a UN food riot.

Town showed up, the party was packed. Danny was circulating with a liter of Bushmills, handing out shots. Beth was spinning music in the living room, old disco and Prince tunes had people shaking their ass.

119

Jennings showed up with some of his homebrew, which unfortunately tasted like it could kill a goat. Kev and Meg brought a case of Guinness and Brian had had himself spray painted green for the night. On the back deck people stayed warm around a blazing chiminea.

When Danny went to the freezer for green jello shots he noticed Turcotte's rig out front. Danny watched. Turcotte cruised by a few times, even stopped once. But never got out of his vehicle. Danny double-checked that the door was locked and went back to the party.

Ed and Amy stopped by and were welcomed by all. Amy got her buzz on and Ed drank tea, looking dapper, chilling in one corner in his leather jacket. At one point Hammer tried to get in but was barred by Pete and Brian, who'd gone for extra ice. Hamilton came by around twelve. He and Danny did a few shots on the back deck.

"I'm planning a little recon mission for tomorrow, first thing."

"Nice," said Danny.

"Think you can find a few folks who wouldn't mind a little back country trip, transportation provided?"

"I think I could find a few volunteers for that kind of mission."

"Nice." They shook hands and Hamilton left before one. Danny told Jen about the mission. They wanted to be fresh for the trip, so they curbed their drinking. In relative terms. That is to say they slowed from Brendan Behan to a mere Dean Martin.

Chapter Sixteen

Danny was shocked when the alarm went off at seven. He'd been asleep for about five seconds. He went to get up and realized he was in his ski clothes. Was the trip already over? This threw him for a moment, but he figured it must have occurred to his drunken brain that this would save time in the morning. At least he hadn't worn his ski boots to bed.

Jen got up too and immediately threw up into the wastebasket. It was touch and go there for a few minutes, but soon they were down on the street out front with their skis when Ed's Pathfinder pulled up. They threw their shit in the back and piled in. He had coffee's waiting for them.

"What's up rock stars?"

"Hey, Ed."

"Thanks for the coffee, Eddie."

"You got it. How are you guys feeling?"

Danny said he was still drunk and didn't mind. Yet. Jen just shook her head.

"So what's the deal with this trip?" asked Ed.

"Hamilton came by the party and told me to get a few volunteers for a secret trip and meet him in the parking lot at eight."

"Good enough."

They drove over to the hill. When they pulled in the parking lot they saw Hamilton pouring gas from a jerry can into the snow cat, which sat up on a trailer behind a big Chevy Suburban. A full size Bronco pulled another four snowmobiles on a second trailer. They hopped out into the chilly dry morning. There was a small group milling around. Brian and Kev, a few guys from ski patrol, a couple of bearded tele skiers they vaguely recognized.

Hamilton jumped up on the cat's tread track and faced the group. "I figured we'd do a little scouting mission this morning. As most of you know, we've applied for a land use permit from the Forest Service to use this place that *that guy* right over there discovered this winter." Danny almost blushed. "So I thought we'd test it out and see how it might work. We're gonna drive up on the Pass, park at the overlook and then double back down the backside and work our way back towards the ski area. This is total trial and error, so I apologize now if you have to wait long times between runs while the cat finds you. But scouting is gonna be important, and soon we're gonna have to start marking a trail map. Because I'm happy to report that as of last night, we have received provisional permission from the Forest Service to open the back country at Winterland."

Yeah!

Woo!

You da man!

Danny and Jen exchanged looks. Ed clapped, most people cheered.

"So I don't know what's gonna happen with Richards, but hopefully he can be talked into letting us still use this space when the sale goes through. But for now, let's head up there and make some turns."

They got back in there cars and soon the little procession was crawling up the Pass towards the overlook. There were snow banks on the sides, but the road was mostly blacktop.

Twenty minutes later they were clicking into skis and agreeing on a rendezvous point. Danny and Ed bumped fists and dropped in. Ed soon got the feel for the deep snow. Up on the Pass it was a more northern exposure and the snow had less exposure to the sun. It still felt powdery, more like winter. They mostly skied in the shade, only popping into the sun near the bottom.

Ed was glad to see he wasn't the last one down. Not that it was a race, but he was a little gun shy on the mountain. He hadn't put in the time that Danny and the others had that winter.

The group formed up at the bottom, a few muffled glove slaps. Soon the cat came grinding up from behind them, and they all piled in. They piled into the padded bench seats in back, the diesel throbbing through, shaking them, and they wound slowly back up the hill. The driver wore noise dampening headphones, but put on a Zeppelin II tape and cranked it for the passengers.

Eight minutes later they had traversed up the hill again at an angle. They unloaded at the top, pulled their skis from metal baskets held to the side of the cat with fresh weld points.

"That was fucking easy," said Danny, smiling. "All this time I've been using my legs like a sucker."

The group dropped in and ripped through the mostly untracked lines. And the scene repeated itself. Danny acted as guide, showing them Hammersmith Palais and the rest. He knew the terrain the best, and they worked across back towards the ski area. By noon they were at Pretty Boy Floyd and the paused for lunch. Hamilton had provided gourmet

122

bologna sandwiches on white bread, and they shut off the cat and left the radio going and had lunch in the warm sun.

Soon they were hiking and catching air off the rock. Buried in winter snow, the drop was down to a manageable eight to ten feet now. Danny landed a 360 on his second try. Jen got off a nice twister, even Ed screwed up his courage and floated off, grabbing his toe side edge, indy-air style. After a bit they loaded back in the cat and continued the journey, Hamilton and a few others buzzing along behind them in the snowmobiles.

It was a fun day, and Danny marveled at the ease of the trip. They easily got twelve runs in, thousands of feet of vertical, and his legs felt fresh. He could see that this business model couldn't miss. The cat dropped them near the top of Mellow Mood and most of them took the short hike through the woods back to the ski area and dropped down the front side. Danny volunteered to go with the cat driver and they worked their way back towards the Pass.

Ed and Jen #2 went down Bullet and worked their way over to the little bar, which Kev and Meg had volunteered to run for the afternoon. There were people hanging out. Many had nursed their hangovers and gotten a late start to the day, but by four there was a good group out there drinking in the sun.

Springtime in the Rockies and Ed was in love. Amy had had to work patrol that day and missed the scouting trip, but she met Ed by the little bar after she did her sweep. She accepted a beer, even in her patrol outfit, which was technically verboten. Then again, her boss was Greg Hamilton, in the running for coolest boss in the world even before he got the land use permit.

Ed didn't charge anyone for beers that day and just basked in the warm light. Amy was on his arm and things were good. Eventually the trailer with the cat on the back pulled in and Hamilton got out to yet another cheer. Ed handed him a cold one.

"That was awesome man, thanks."

"You got it Ed, glad to have you out there with us."

Hamilton accepted some more congratulations, word had spread that the land use permit had come through. Everyone was handing him beers and patting him on the back when Ed pulled him aside.

"Dude, that was major. That is a fucking goldmine back there. You could make a killing."

"I know. I was pretty good, huh? I just wish I could cash in on it. All this time I was running the hill I never thought about letting people ski back there. Hell, I didn't even know about it." He smile faded. "The only problem is it's too little too late."

"So that's definite, you're gonna sell to Richards?"

"I haven't got much choice. Supposedly he's gonna make a lot of improvements, turn the hill around. In some ways I hate to lose the place, but the debt is just killing me. I know it seems like there's a lot of new people in town, on the hill and everything. Which is true. But it's still not that profitable. It would take time to get the cat operation up and running, that would probably bring in the crowds, but I just haven't got time. I have to sell by April first. It's etched in stone."

"What about Jennings? He told me he started a Winterland defense fund."

"Yeah, I heard he's raised almost nine hundred dollars so far. Its great and all, I appreciate the help. Every time I see a SAVE WINTERLAND sticker on some pick up truck I get choked up. But what can I do? I'm obligated by the corporation documents to take the highest bid, Richards is the only bidder and I can *not* get any more time from the bank."

Ed shook his head. What a shame. "'Least let me buy you another beer."

"That I can afford." Hamilton accepted the beer and joined the rest of the party.

Ed walked a little ways from everyone, a funny look on his face. He was just staring up at the hill.

***

LIVE WIRE for MARCH 18, 1999

This is the winter of our discontent. Wake up, Winterland! Stop the bamboozle from the south. While an oleaginous Texas con man threatens to gut our town, why do we line up like sheep to the slaughter? Rage, rage against the dying of the light.

For those of you who haven't been following the scrum, let me hip you to some new shinola. We all know Greggie, we know what kind of guy he is. So he's in a bind? Bank closing in like Gestapo? And we talk about real estate values. About selling out. This nut, "Nut" Richards promises change, improvements, the all inclusive term—infrastructure. Ha! This is a fast talking used car salesman.

For those of you with short memories let me refresh you. For generations his was a vivid town with a strong tradition of ranching. Then when Cody Hammer and his team had a few bad years the vultures were circling. Then they called it a Real Estate Investment Trust. I called it a leveraged rip off. We had some other high rollers from Pure Aggro Tejas, only this time they were from Dallas, where our good buddy Nut is from Houston. Big difference. Like between a cobra and a mongoose.

The so called "trust" bought out the cattle yard, with big promises of reform this, streamline that. Efficiency! Profitability! Let me tell you friends, they streamlined it right out of business. Broke it up and sold the parts off like a swap shop. You know people who lost their jobs, their houses, their sense of pride and self determination. You know these people. You are these people. I am these people. We all suffered.

This is the same deal in a different decade. This bag of hot air wants to buy out Greggie and turn Winterland into a theme park for the wealthy elite. Make Aspen seem like a lemonade stand. Meanwhile Klein and his ilk are stumbling drunk with dollar sign eyeballs. I say hang em high!

This is an old west showdown. We got a new sheriff in town—not literally, unfortunately. Our good Sheriff Turcotte is a busy man. Cut him some slack! Its hard work beating up hippies and shutting down profitable, community supported enterprises just because his corporate pay master Klein doesn't like it! Wither Greggie? I say give your money to the Winterland Defense Fund. Donations are being accepted at the Wire offices, at the lift ticket window. Let's work together and preserve our funky little town before its too late. If not, get ready for condo sprawl and soaring rentals that will price the vibrancy of this town right out. Just like they did in Vail. Just like they did in Telluride. Keep Winterland Weird!

Rage, rage against the dying of the light.

I know many of you want to sell. You've had some tough times, many of you have lost homes and businesses. But I say let Greggie stay on. If anyone can make this hill profitable, the right way, its him. Then your land values will come back and you can have your cake.

This land is your land. And you can sell your land. You just shouldn't have to sell your soul to do it.

Do not go gentle into that goodnight.

—Humbly yours, Kent Jennings.

***

Hamilton read the editorial when he got home. For the first time in years, he broke down. He cried, feeling responsible for all these people. He felt sick. How could he sell out now? It wasn't just him that was affected, it was the whole town, the very nature of the community. He would have given anything for a way out. But he couldn't think of a single fucking thing he could do about it.

Part Four
Co-Op City, Boogie Down

Chapter Seventeen

It was a restless night all over Winterland. Many people got less sleep than Hamilton. It also snowed. Not a ton, eight inches or so, but enough for fresh tracks in the morning. Jennings was drinking gin and passed out with his feet near the coal stove and burned one of the soles on his Army boots. It smoldered all night even while his editorial burned a new resolve into the soul of the town. In the morning, and rare for spring, it was a bluebird day.

Ed didn't fall asleep til dawn. Around eight Amy woke him from fitful dreams and they made out for a while before she had to leave for work. All morning he seethed. He had to do something.

***

Ed had lunch at the Tres Hermanas, then headed over to the hill. He'd just set out the tip bucket, newly rededicated to the Winterland Defense Fund in black magic marker, and was about to tap the keg when he felt a heavy hand on his shoulder.

"Punk!" The last thing Ed saw was Turcotte's ugly face, then the truncheon smashed down across his face. He collapsed unconscious, with drops of blood staining the snow.

"He was resisting," said Turcotte to his deputy, who nodded. They carried Easy Ed to the squad car and flung him in the back. Few had seen the attack. They were busy. It was a powder day.

***

Around back, by the holding cells, they dropped Ed in a heap. He was still out cold.

"If he tries to get up, break his ribs. Teach you to fool with me, punk." Turcotte went around to open the cell from the inside while the deputy watched him.

Turcotte opened up and they dragged Ed in, letting him drop on the cement floor. Turcotte and the deputy went up to the office.

"OK, male Caucasian…write this down!" The deputy grabbed an arrest report form. "Male Caucasian, twenty-two years old. Edward

Ellsworth Stallings of Grosse Point Michigan. Florida's driver's license. Conspiracy to violate state liquor laws, operating an establishment that knowingly sold intoxicating sprits to minors, operating without a liquor license and resisting arrest."

***

Ed came around slowly. His face was busted. He touched his nose and almost threw up it hurt so bad. He tried to get up, but it hurt too much. He went back to sleep, hoping he was dead.

His dreams were jagged fragments. He'd be in the cell, then up in the ski cat, then down at Trappers. Eventually he hauled himself up on the cold metal bench. He was shivering, only vaguely able to think…

Punk!…bluebird…liquor…license…Amy…Danny…Amy… head…hurts…why?...hurts…Winterland…ski…powder…jennings… can I get some cooperation?......... cooperation!.......hurts……turcotte….. dick…….Trappers……..ski…..cooperation…..ski….hinterland…ski… get some cooperation….co-operation…

***

Pete and Brian had been making turns on Straight Shot, ripping through the last spring freshies, and felt like a beer around three.

"Let's just go down for a quick one, then catch a few more lifts."

"Maybe a couple quick ones, then a lift. Then the shrine."

"I like the way you think." The skied down to the hay bales, which were deserted.

"That's odd, what time is it?" They were about to go back up when they saw the blood in the snow.

"Oh, shit."

***

…..ski corporation….bluebird…ski…Hinterland….corporation… ski…corporation. cooperation…corporation…cooperation…ski cooperation…cooperation…co-op…ski cooperation…co-op…ski co-op….Ski Co-Op! Ski Co-Op!

***

Danny was just dropping a few napkins in a sack of burritos for a customer when they burst into Tres.

"Danny, its Ed."

130

"Well, we think its Ed."

"There was blood all over the snow by the plywood stand, and no sign of him."

"We think maybe he got robbed for the bucket."

"Yeah," said Danny. "Or maybe Turcotte came back with reinforcements."

Danny immediately called the station.

"Sheriff's Department, this call is being recorded."

"Are you holding an Ed Stallings?"

"Who's calling, please?"

Danny was about to answer, then momentarily heard Turcotte in the background, then the phone was muffled.

"What is the nature of this call, please?"

"You know God damn well what the nature is, are you—ahh fuck this!" He slammed the phone down and they ran out front. He called up the stairs. "Jen! I'm taking the Tres van!"

"OK. Where?"

"They got Ed!" And the three of them peeled out.

***

Danny had calmed, slightly, by the time they got to the station.

"It is possible that they're not even holding him."

"Not likely, I can feel it. Ed hasn't missed a day since he opened that stand. And the blood? They got him, Turcotte is just probably pissed about us showing him up the other day."

"Yeah, there's bad blood going back to Trappers."

They rushed in.

"Can we speak to Turcotte?"

"I'm sorry, Sheriff Turcotte is in a meeting, can I help you?"

"Yeah, have you got Ed in the tank?"

"I'm sorry prisoner lists are not public information until they are arraigned."

Danny glared at the deputy, who wasn't much older than him. "Give me a fucking break. You used to come into Trappers. Is Ed here or not?" The guy softened, slightly.

"All right, off the record…they got him downstairs. We'll make sure he gets his phone call. He's all right. I saw him. Not pretty, but all right."

"Thanks, man."

They left and drove up to Jennings's. They found him drinking a bottle of his lousy beer. He seemed jolly.

"Mornin, boys."

"Its five o'clock."

"PM?"

"Kent, they got Ed. Turcotte's holding him. I think he might be beat up, too."

"That pig fucking fascist! Well, we gotta go bail him out."

"We tried that, they won't even let us see him. I don't even think he's been able to make a phone call."

A dark look crossed Jennings's face. "That editorial must have pissed Turcotte off."

"Don't worry, the editorial was fucking brilliant."

"Yeah, its all anyone on the hill was talking about."

"Yeah, plus we had a little run in with him on St. Pats. I may have called him a pig behind his back," said Danny.

"Well, Danny, Alexander Hamilton established that you can't be convicted of libel for printing the truth."

***

When Amy got home she shed her patrol uniform and was about to jump in the shower when she saw the light blinking on the answering machine. The minute she heard the voice she knew it was bad.

"Amy, it's me. I'm at the Sheriff department. I got hit on the top of the face, by the front. I can't make bail until they arraign me..in court. Call Jennings. I love you." She started to cry. She called the Wire. No Jennings. She got dressed and rushed down to Tres, the girls let her in and they had some tea in the kitchen. Outside the temperature was dropping as the sun went down.

***

The boys got into it. Jennings opened his closets, and they got ragged up in prison break clothes, old military uniforms mostly. Since they knew Ed was basically all right, their anger had subsided. They were just in for a bit of lark. They weren't so sure about Jennings. While they were getting dressed, he'd been sharpening his Bowie knife. Before they left he strapped a machete to his belt and tucked a pistol in the small of his back.

"That's a fake gun, right Jennings?"

132

He just laughed.

By nine o'clock they rolled back down through the compound with the headlights off, down towards the town. Danny had the hastily painted banner folded on his lap. This was gonna be fun. They bounced in anticipation.

"Just make as much noise as possible. I'll handle the rest." Jennings's face was maniacal, lit in ghostly profile now by only the dashboard glare and his unfiltered Camel.

***

Deputy Smith was on desk duty, and was almost finished the crossword when he heard the commotion. Chris Mankin, the Wire's photo editor, was out front with his camera, like Jennings had asked. He started popping his flash when the boys rushed the station house.

"Free Dexter Bradley! Free Dexter Bradley!"

"Who do we want?"

"Bradley!"

"When do we want him?"

"Now!"

Smith didn't know what to make of this. He called Turcotte. Danny, Pete and Brian were all over the lobby, jumping up and down, shouting at the top of their lungs, banging on the desk, throwing staplers around, dumping stacks of paper. Just as Turcotte walked out of his office, they unfurled a huge banner.

"What the hell is this?" Danny saw Turcotte reach for his truncheon, but he didn't draw it. Yet. His rage was tempered by a genuine bewilderment.

"What the good Christ is this?"

"Let Dexter Bradley go free, you bastard!"

***

From his cell Ed heard the commotion. He wondered what was going on, he was the only one being held.

Then sotto voce in the dark: "Stallings. Stallings, you in there?"

"Who's there?"

"Collect call."

"Jennings! What's going on? Who's Dexter Bradley?"

"It's from a Dylan song, never mind. Just to confuse that fuck. What's happening, what are they holding you for?"

133

"I have no idea. Turcotte whacked me in the face for selling beer."

"Bastard. We'll have him up on brutality charges before you can say Chicago 8. Wait till I call my attorney."

"Never mind that, I'm all right," Ed could hear someone coming down the stairs now. The protest was losing momentum. "Jennings, I've got it. We take the hill private. We make it a co-op. Sell shares, the town people can buy them. The skiers. Business owners. We all buy them, I don't know, thousand bucks apiece. We can outbid this Richards fuck. We can buy the hill ourselves and keep it alive, then open Hinterland and rebuild with the profits from that."

A smile creased Jennings weathered face. The boy was good. "I'll tell Hamilton. You hang tight, we'll get you out of here."

Then Jennings heard Turcotte barking. "Stallings! Front and center!" Jennings slunk back into the night and jogged to the rendezvous.

In the lobby Smith and Wilkins were shoving the boys out.

"Get the hell out of here, you dirty long hairs."

"Free Dexter Bradley!" They tried to get the chant going, but it was just too funny now. They were shaking with excitement and giddy laughter. They ran back towards the van.

Smith noticed the banner on the ground. "What do you suppose that's supposed to mean?"

"I don't know, lets get back inside, it's freezing out here."

Crumpled on the ground was an old sheet with a spray painted slogan: SIC SEMPER TYRANNIS.

***

They parked the van on B Street and headed up the stairs. They'd offered to drop Jennings off, but he was rolling now, talking a mile a minute in between slugs from a cheap gallon of red wine. They entered the apartment.

"The fuck?"

"What, are you guys storming the Bastille?"

"Oh, the gets ups, I almost forgot. Well, we did storm the Sheriff's department."

"How's Ed? Did you see him?"

"He's fine, Amy, don't worry," said Danny. "Jennings talked to him, he's fine. We figure he'll make bail in the morning."

Jennings staggered to the center of the room. "They can't hold him. Habeas corpus! Sit down everyone [they were already seated] and I'll tell you what Ed told me. Anyone want some wine?"

"NO."

"All right, take it easy." He glugged the wine. "Ed had a very interesting idea that just might change things and get this nut case Richards off our back. Check it out."

***

Hamilton got the call about twenty minutes later. He headed over to Tres, and saw Kev and Meg on Main Street, heading the same way.

"What's happening man?"

"What's the rhubarb? Jennings just called me, I could barely understand him."

"Danny called us, said Ed's got a plan to save the hill."

"…Really?"

They arrived at the restaurant and climbed the stairs to the apartment, where they found the others. Jennings was out cold.

"What happened to him?" asked Kev.

"The usual," said Danny.

"So what's the big miracle?" Asked Hamilton.

"Now, this is Ed's idea, and Jennings helped flesh it out, he was screaming his head off for a while, the Sandinistas, the French Revolution, it was quite a performance. Then he passed out and we put him on the couch. Anyway, Ed was saying, we make it into a co-op. Winterland. We make it like a community thing. We sell shares, and anyone can buy them," said Danny.

"How would that work?" said Hamilton, his brow was wrinkled.

Jen #1 was punching numbers into her calculator. "How much do you owe the bank? If you don't mind me asking."

"I don't mind. I just checked. One million, one hundred seventeen thousand and change."

"And how much is Richards offering?"

"He offered one-point two-two."

"So that will leave you free and clear?"

"Yeah, that will clear my debt, and hopefully have a little left over to put a down payment on a house in town. But Richards Oil would own the hill."

"So we need to come up with one point one, whatever."

"Well, no" said Hamilton. "We would need to outbid Richards. I have a clause in my mortgagee document that requires me to sell to the highest bidder."

"So that's what we have to come up with?"

"That's….twelve hundred and twenty shares we need to sell," said Jen #1.

"That's not that many," said Danny.

"Yes it is. It's an awful lot," said Hamilton.

"Yeah, and we only have, what? Nine days to do this?" asked Kev.

"Yeah, I am required to sell on April 1, I've already signed papers to legally put in on the market."

"Well, shit man, I'll buy a share right now," said Danny. "I might be able to buy two."

"Well, that's the thing, Jennings was saying, before he—" they looked at Jennings, snoring on the couch a few feet away. "You have to be careful to only let people buy one share, or they could just get bought out by some big whale," said Jen #2.

"Yeah, if that's the case, anyone could just scoop them up. Even Richards," said Meg.

"Well, let's do it like…fractional ownership or whatever," said Danny. "Like you can buy one share, but you can't buy multiple shares. You can put more money in, but you still only get one vote on the board."

"Yeah, that's good."

"So what's to stop Richards, or any other high roller, from just buying all twelve hundred shares just to control the board?"

"Well, we could make the board meet here in town. There would be like a charter document, that would prohibit a single owner, and we could have this drafted by an attorney, that requires the board to meet once a month, here in Winterland, not in Houston or LA or whatever. One share, one vote." Said Hamilton.

"Right, so if Richards, or anyone else, wanted to fuck with us, he'd have to not only buy all the shares, but fly twelve hundred separate people up here every month to vote," said Brian.

"Yeah, that way, say someone like—I mean, I know my old roommate Dab would give us some money. He makes bank. And like even if he gives us like five grand, he still gets one share and one vote. He gets maybe I guess he gets like a bigger piece of the pie, like an equity position in the company because he put more money in, but still, it's just the one vote."

"Yeah, you run it like a non-profit," said Jen #2. They were flying now, the room sparked with energy.

"Totally. All the profits get poured back into the company, then we use that make improvements," said Beth.

136

"And I can...I mean, the board can...use that to open the backcountry, and build some housing units near the base area. Then with the ski cat operation, we lure in the steep and deep crowd," said Hamilton.

"Yeah, absolutely," said Danny. "We charge a bit more for the cat tour, like, eighty bucks or something, which is still a steal."

"Yeah, and with some housing and a better lodge, we'd get more people up here. I always wanted to make improvements, I just never had the cash. We'll have to market to a different kind of skier. Forget the families, they aren't coming up here anyway. We go after the steep and deep crowd. We go after the same guys that go helicopter skiing in Alaska. I mean, a day of heli skiing is twelve hundred bucks, most ski cat tours run about two-fifty a day. We'd have the best deal anywhere," said Hamilton.

"Oh my God, this could *so* work you guys," said Amy.

"Well, we've got nine days is the only thing," said Hamilton. "I love this idea, in fact I love all of you people. I don't know if we can pull this off, but let's really try. I hate the idea of selling out to some rich asshole who's gonna ruin this place. Let's do it. Lets fucking really do this thing."

Yeah!

"OK, so I guess at this point, we go our separate ways. Everyone check their bank balance, empty out the couch, pennies in the ashtray, whatever. Call your friends, beg your parents. Whatever it takes, we've got twelve hundred shares to sell and no time to do it," said Jen #2.

"We meet back here at five tomorrow," said Hamilton.

"Let's get giggin."

* * *

Hamilton didn't sleep that night. He woke his lawyer up about two am and ran it by him. The lawyer was groggy—and a little pissed off—but soon came around and told Greg that he thought it could work. It was radical and risky, but he couldn't see any legal reason they couldn't do it. Hamilton made him promise to buy a share before he let him go back to sleep.

* * *

Turcotte woke Ed with a night stick smashed against the bars, a clanging echo rattling him awake. Ed was shivering uncontrollably. Turcotte entered the cell, unlocked the external door and told Ed to beat it.

"You'll get a summons to appear in district court in Milner. If I catch you so much as *drinking* beer in this town, you're gonna be right back in here. You got that?"

"Get fucked." Ed went out into the cold and started to walk back home. When he got to Main Street he looked as his reflection in a shop window. His nose was swollen, with an ugly cut across the bridge. Two black eyes. But otherwise he wasn't too bad. His head hurt like hell and he was still a little dizzy, but mostly he was cold. When he got home Amy just held onto to him. She only let go to heat up some soup.

"We had a meeting at Tres Hermanas last night. We're gonna try and do the co-op."

"Oh yeah? Awesome. That is awesome. Can we just go to bed? I don't think I've ever been so cold."

***

In the morning Danny checked the bank. He had fourteen hundred in there, and another few hundred in burrito tips saved in a coffee can. Beth, Jen and Jen each agreed to buy shares and to pretty much empty their company account into the fund, about twelve thousand dollars worth. Kev and Meg bought shares. Pete and Brian between them had almost eighty-three dollars, but promised to work as tireless fundraisers. Ed didn't have much—the Miami money was long gone—but the little bar singles and quarters added up to about a grand. He offered to sell his Pathfinder to raise more funds. Amy had an expensive necklace from her ex that she was gonna sell anyway. Everyone scraped and dug, came up with everything they could, called friends and looked forward to the meeting at five.

***

Over at Tres, the girls were standing around the couch, unsure of what to do.

"You wake him up."

"I'm not going *near* that guy. You brought him here."

"Danny brought him here, but he's at the bank."

"I am not touching that guy."

"Hey. Hey, mister?" Jennings stirred. He grumbled.

"Sorry to wake you, mister, but could you—"

Jennings ripped a wet fart.

"I refuse to believe that this is happening right now."

138

They met at Tres. After one day of fundraising they had sold forty one shares. Not that they had shares to sell, yet, technically.

"My lawyer is working on the document, we're gonna get share certificates printed up, but it's gonna take a few days. Right now we're just asking people to trust us," said Hamilton.

"So far, so good" said Jen #1. She punched numbers on the little calculator and came up with a number. "We've sold forty one hypothetical shares, and raised almost fifty three thousand dollars, including the additional buy ins and the Winterland Defense Fund from the Wire."

"That's awesome," said Danny. "Fifty grand overnight, amazing."

"Yeah, but that's not gonna make the nut," said Hamilton.

"Yeah, not even close. At that rate"—she punched numbers—"we'd need to raise that much money every day for almost a month. And we have nine, no…eight days left. Plus now we're personally all tapped out."

Just then Ed and Amy rolled in. Everyone turned to see, and the Tres girls took turns hugging him.

"I'm all right, seriously. Thanks you guys."

"I hate that fucker," said Danny.

"Don't worry about him. Well, I heard you're already selling shares, that is amazing. Amy and I will buy one each, and I'm gonna sell my truck to raise more money" said Ed. "How much do we have right now?"

"About fifty three, well now, fifty five thousand," said Jen #1.

"So just one million point one million to go, huh?" said Ed. Who could he ask for money? He thought about the old man, and if he could get him to—no! Forget it, he'd do this himself or not at all. "We can do this. I spoke to Jennings, he's gonna pretty much turn this week's Wire into an ad for the Co-Op, he thinks maybe his publisher will kick some in. He also said that if we do it as a non-profit, people might be able to make their contributions tax deductible."

"That would be huge," said Hamilton.

Danny said, "so we'll have Drunky McDrunk Drunk fill up the paper with ad copy, we can put up posters around town, ask all the businesses for donations. What else?"

"Has anyone got any rich friends?" asked Hamilton.

"Muni desk, Horowitz."

"Dab."

"Danny! What's happening, my man?"

"You got a second?"

"Yeah, the bond market closed twenty minutes ago. What's up?"

"Dab, I got a major situation here. Remember how I said this town is like struggling financially, and the hill was about to go under and everything?"

"Yeah, the oil cowboy's gonna buy it, right?"

"Yeah, the butt nut. Well, that's the thing. We might be able to buy it ourselves. We're starting this co-op. You know, to purchase the mountain from this local guy here who's underwater. But we've only got like a week left. That way the cowboy dude doesn't get his hands on it and turn it into a Lear Jet parking lot, you know?"

"The People's Republic of Winterland, huh? Did you get Karl Marx to sign off on this deal?"

"Yeah, but Adam Smith said it was a go, too." They laughed.

"So like, we're selling shares, thousand bucks a pop. I know you'll be interested, right?"

"What do I get for my thousand?"

"What you don't get is your ass whipped by me."

"Go on."

"But seriously, you buy one share, it's a thousand dollars, and you can do more, some people are doing more, but you still just get one share per person. And then you get a vote on the board, and I think probably discounts on a season pass, we haven't really figured that out yet. But everyone who buys shares, you'll be like a limited partner in the company."

"Yeah, man, I'll do it. Of course. I've been meaning to do some skiing anyway, just can't seem to get away. Matter of fact, let me talk to the other traders, these knuckleheads right here, see if we can't sell a few more of your little Das Kapital. Let me call you back."

"You think those dudes are gonna be interested?"

"Are you kidding? I've seen these guys drop a G in a strip club bathroom. I'll tell them you're offering an arbitrage opportunity on a private equity placement…they'll be on it like a pack of jackals. Let me call you back."

***

From this tiny mountain hamlet, furious calls buzzed down the phone lines to distant lands. In a few days checks started to roll in. From

LA, from Nantucket, from Mountain Lakes, New Jersey and from old fraternity brothers and from dudes you barely remembered from the show at the Cow Palace. Parents wrote checks, buddies sent twenty bucks. Neighbors and cousins passed the hat at bingo, at the office, at the building site.

***

Jennings was slumped at his desk at The Wire Wednesday night when his boss approached. Jennings looked like hell. He hadn't slept in a week. (He'd passed out plenty, just hadn't slept.) And from the smell, hadn't bathed either. The publisher almost held his nose. He had Jennings's copy in his hand.

"Is this stuff accurate?"

"Cross checked and attributed. It is air tight."

"Good work."

***

The Wire came out on Thursday. There was a long story on Ed. The headline was "Corruption, Police Brutality in Sheriff's Office." It detailed Turcotte's history with Ed, his cozy business relationship with Klein, raised the possibility of illegal campaign contributions, talked about the closing of Trappers and the trumped up liquor charges. They had a picture of Ed on the front page, his face swollen. Jennings had had Mankin use the Frankenstein mug shot technique, where they used a bounce flash off the ceiling to give the image a garish shadow. Ed looked like the guy in a hostage video.

***

LIVE WIRE for MARCH 25, 1999

This is it boys and girls. We have a chance to make something happen, and I do mean now! Less than one week. By now you've heard about the Winterland Ski Co-Op. What Greggie and the boys are trying to do is an eleventh hour end run, a ninth inning Hail Mary, a mixed metaphor like nobody's business. Take this sucker private.

Think about it. The mountain, owned by the town, for the benefit of the people.

Buy a share, buy one for your dog. Just get the money into Co-Op coffers by one week from today.

I do not plan to be around for that, as I fear that Mussolini Turcotte will have stomped me into a grease spot by then. But it will be a great day when the flag of freedom flies over Winterland, and the ski hill profits drive the town's economy like the glory days of the cattle yard.

You want to sell your business? What better time than in an expanding economy that's sure to follow a home grown renaissance? You want to ski powder, dude? What better place than on a mountain that you own. You wanna trump some chump from Texas, be my guest. The people have spoken. The Co-Op is the way.

You can be part of something to tell your grandkids about. You can tell them you were there, during our darkest hour, manning the barricades. To paraphrase old Billy Wordsworth, bliss it was on that dawn to be alive, but to be young was very heaven.

Don't serve the machine. Don't accept corporate control and the soul deadening monoculture. There's millions being made overnight in so-called Silicon Valley, but we've got a chance to do something right here in the Arapahoe Valley. Lets do something permanent, something that—guess what?—Bingo!—will make money. But make money the right way, for the benefit of the many, and not the few. Ski bum retreat, not wealthy elite. Power to the—ahh! You get the idea. I hope.

Support Greggie and the Co-Op. Strike out, boys, for the hill!

—Humbly yours, Kent Jennings.

***

In the big glass tower at One Financial Place, Houston Texas, U.S. of A., Nut Richards was getting excited. It wouldn't be long now.

He already had this little nymphet under the desk and she was about to get started.

"You be gentle now Stacy. Don't forget I'm considering you for a big promotion."

"It's Tracy."

"It duddn't really matter."

"Mr. Richards, call on line one."

"Not now, Bernice!"

"It's Greg Hamilton."

"Oh, fer chrissakes, put him through."

"Mr. Richards? It's Greg Hamilton."

"What can I do for you, Greg? I'm a little busy." He winked at Stacy (Tracy).

"I was speaking with my attorney, and he's advised me that, ah, legally, I have to put the mountain up for a public auction. Its, ah, part of ownership charter, apparently, I wasn't aware of it, but yeah, apparently there has to be a 24-hour window where we're accepting bids." Hamilton winced a little on his end, hoping the guy didn't explode.

"Well, hell (wail hail) I don't see what difference it makes. "Less a course you got some other interested parties that I don't know about."

"I can honestly say at this point yours is the only offer, and that, on that conference call between you and my lawyer and Mr. Degbert, you recall, at that point I had to disclose to you that I am contractually obligated to sell to the highest bidder. And that remains true as well."

"Well, that's fine then. You know this ain't my first time at the rodeo." Richards wasn't worried about any public auction. Degbert had set aside close to twenty million dollars already in the war chest. He was ready to start this turkey shoot. "Still April first, right?"

"Yeah, that twenty four hour period, on April first."

"Wail hail, you'll get my fax then. Talk to you later, Greg. Hey, where the hail...?"

***

Tracy was already in the elevator, checking the help wanted page in the Chronicle.

Chapter Eighteen

More money was coming in every day. It was gonna be close. By Wednesday they had about eight hundred thousand dollars collected, but donations had started to ebb. Ed got a check for twenty thousand dollars from Miller. In the memo line it just said "do the right thing."

Danny and Jen #2 took a break from the stress of the fundraising for a rare day on the hill. It barely snowed anymore, and everyday it got warmer the sun melted a few tons of snow off the hill and washed it down into the ground; into the Arapahoe River; into the Colorado River; into the Pacific Ocean.

They skied in t-shirts and jeans, sluicing through the heavy snow that formed into tiny balls the locals called chowder snow. It was sloppy and fun and wet. At the base there were puddles you could skim across if you kept your speed.

Danny and Jen #2 fell and laughed, visited the shrine and skied some more. By three thirty they were down at the hay bale bar.

Ed was looking better. He had just a small bandage on his nose now. No one had seen Turcotte since The Wire had come out, and word around town was that the DA was launching an investigation. They drained a few brews, then headed back home.

Back at the green and white Victorian, Danny found a Fed Ex envelope with a Chicago postmark. Inside was a check for close to sixty thousand dollars and the names of eighteen people on the equity and fixed income trading desks at Burnham, Brandt who wanted to buy shares. He quietly said "thanks, Dab" to himself.

***

When Degbert heard about the public auction he exploded.

"Why didn't you tell me about this?"

"I don't think it makes any difference."

"Nut, of course it makes a difference. What if word gets out about the auction? We'll have every real estate speculator from here to Timbuktu trying to crash the party. Not to mention if Vail Resorts or Intrawest hear

145

about it! The beauty of this deal is that we're the only player in the game. If we lose that edge, the deal gets a whole lot less sexy."

"Don't worry, we'll win the bid. Didn't you tell me we have almost twenty million in the Galveston account now?"

"Yeah, but at a certain point, the deal gets less attractive. We do not want to get in a bidding war. I'm calling Hamilton's counsel right now. There's no way I'm letting this happen."

Degbert was so upset it started Nut to thinking. He looked out the big glass window and started to worry.

***

With two days to go they had their daily meeting at Tres Hermanas. Jen #1 had worked tirelessly, and now had every penny accounted for on spreadsheets. She and Hamilton sat at the kitchen table, running numbers. Hamilton's lawyer had finally gotten the physical shares printed, so locals were stopping by his office and signing affidavits and walking away—at least on paper—with partial ownership shares in the Co-Op. Some people hid them in safe deposit boxes at the bank, some hung them over the fireplace. In an unfortunate incident after having twenty pints of lager, Jennings used his for toilet paper.

Ed and Amy were enjoying one of her rare days off and stayed in all day.

"So what's the total, Jen?" asked Hamilton.

"We have, as of today's mail and all collections from the Defense Fund...eight-hundred forty three thousand, nine hundred forty-seven dollars and eleven cents."

"Shit. That's great, but I don't know what else we can do," said Hamilton. Jen #2 looked worried. Danny was getting that old feeling, the calm amidst chaos. He didn't know how it was gonna work, but he had a good feeling. He may have been the only one.

"I've asked everyone I know, people who barely remember me. I don't have any more phone calls I can make."

"What about the bank, Greg, maybe you could just borrow more against he future profits?" asked Beth.

"The bank has a hit squad out looking for me right now. They already fronted me a bridge loan for fifty large, which I poured back into the company and employee bonuses. They won't touch me."

Danny went out onto the deck, already in the shade at this late afternoon hour. It was a little chilly, he was handed a bomber joint by

Wardo, who'd stopped by with a check from his sponsor for fifteen hundred bucks.

"This Co-Op is getting big news. Free Skier Magazine called me, they're gonna send a photographer out. It'll be my first national exposure."

"That's awesome Wardo, congrats, man." said Danny. "This thing has really gotten big. I think Jen said we've gotten contributions from thirty-seven states or something. It's wild."

"Oh yeah, that reminds me, I got a check from Framingham," said Brian.

"Oh, your old ski buddy?"

"Yeah, he lives out in San Fran now. He was doing something with computers last I heard. It's such a waste, he was a pretty good skier. Loved to party. Loved this stuff." Brian handed Danny the joint. Mostly smoked down, it was now merely the size of a roll of quarters.

"Yeah, remind me to grab that check, it's over at our place, still in the envelope."

"You got it, Brian."

***

"Bitterroot and Platte, may I help you?"

"May I speak with Matt Platte please, tell him it's Michael Degbert from Richards Oil."

"One moment please."

"This is Platte."

"Platte, Michael Degbert. What's this public auction horse shit? I thought we had an agreement in place."

"At this point my client has agreed in writing only to put the property up for sale on a specified date, and that will take place on April first."

"OK, we're flexible on the date, that's fine, but there's no way it can be a 24 hour auction. If word leaks we'll have a stampede, and that's not in either of our interests."

"It might be in my client's."

"We've already committed due diligence on this project, as you know I've flown up there I don't know how many times personally, and we have contractors lined up, ready to break ground on a multi-million-dollar development package. If some fly-by-night horse trader gets wind of this auction, there's no guarantee that they will have the resources nor the expertise to handle a deal of this scope and complexity. I'm saying it's in all of our interest to see that this is handled right, and by a major

147

player like Richards Oil. Therefore we feel that a simple one hour, closing window auction is the best bet."

"Give us two hours and you have a deal."

"Fine."

"OK, so let's say that from two to four pm on Friday, April 1, 1999 we have an unadvertised but public auction for the ownership of the Winterland Ski Area. I will be present at the Winterland corporate offices (read: Quonset hut) with an independent auditor from the Wells Fargo bank and a notary public to certify the bids as they come in. Fair?"

"Fair enough. You'll get our offer just after two."

***

Ed stripped line and got ready to retrieve. He was using a different fly than his usual Clouser. A lightweight faux-danny boy that he'd tied himself from a pattern Jennings showed him. It took some getting used to, it was so light it barely had the heft to cast. But Ed had good touch, he got the line working, loading the rod, the line curving out in sweeping parabolas. The thread-like leader almost invisible in the still early morning light, the steam rising from the river.

He felt a tug, let the fish take the hook, wary of breaking it off. He let the fish drift a bit more with the current, then yanked up, setting the hook.

Vvvvvvrrrrrr!

The reel started whirring, dumping line as the steelhead raced for cover. He was heading for a boulder downstream. Quickly into his backing, Ed only had about thirty yards to spare, then twenty, then ten. He grabbed the spinning fly reel, bruising his knuckle and at length, managed to turn the fish. The rod alive! Jumping! He got a few cranks on the reel, picking up the bow in the line, and the fish made its first jump. Bright reds and brown spots danced in the light refracting from his initial splash. Ed kept the rod tip up, bending, applying pressure, and got a crank or two when he could. Slowly he regained line. Most of the backing was reloaded now, then the floating line came into the reel. He worked, never jerking the fish, staying patient.

His heart dropped when he felt the line go slack. But a few more cranks revealed the fish still made fast. He'd just been swimming back upstream, slacking the line. Ed hauled when he could, let the fish take line when it wanted. Always working, always tiring.

The fish made a dramatic tail walk, exploding through the swirling current just twenty feet in front of Ed, shaking its head in fight for life. Ed nursed the fish closer, a few more cranks, and landed it.

He held the trout in his hands, saw it gasping for breath, its gills working, its pointy jaw held the feathery lure in one corner.

Ed whispered to the fish.

"Good luck."

Then removed the hook and held the fish underwater. He moved it back and forth to get water moving over its gills, and the fish revived. It blew out of his grip with a mighty tail whip and swam into the deep water, still heading for the protection behind the big rock. Ed smiled in the wispy morning light, then turned back towards the mountain and started to walk home.

***

After Ed got home and hosed off his fishing gear Amy had a little time before her patrol shift. They made out on the couch and quickly succumbed, the attraction between them so palpable it colored the air in the room. Ed felt warm in the heaven of her eyes.

Then Ed threw on some shorts and got the skillet going and made her a fried egg sandwich with cheddar to eat on the way to work. After she left he put on a sweater and went and sat in a low-slung chair on the back deck. Still barefoot he had a coffee and looked up at the mountain, bright with spring's redolent show.

He had done what he could. Emptied his pockets, the hay bale bar profits, every cent in the world into the Co-Op fund. It didn't seem like they were gonna do it. They were maxed out and still short by hundreds of thousands of dollars with a day to go. But he was all right. He knew he had done everything, that he had helped. He had, finally, and for the first time in his life, given everything to something bigger than himself.

***

That night at Tres, the mood was somber. They added and re-added the numbers, and it wasn't that close. They had about nine-hundred and something, which was astonishing for a slap ass, half baked idea that occurred only a week earlier to a beat up guy in jail. But it wasn't gonna be enough. Nut had already officially bid one point two, there was no reason to think that he wouldn't again at the auction the next day.

Then Brian burst in waving a check around.

"We got it! We got it!"

"You got what?" asked Hamilton, trying not to get overly excited. It was hard, Brian's energy was manic.

"How much is it?" asked Jen #2.

"Check it out, my man." He handed Hamilton a check.

***

Nut was about to leave for the day. He'd play golf, then take some party girls out for a night on the town. That morning he'd dispatched Degbert to Winterland to oversee the bid process and make sure there was no funny business. He planned to spend the next day out on the Viking.

Bernice caught him just before he got on the elevator.

"There's a collect call sir, from Winterland."

"I don't give a shit."

"The guy says he's got some information that might be useful to you."

"Tell him to speak to Degbert. He should be on the ground within the hour."

"He said there's another interested party. A local one, up there." Nut took the call at Bernice's desk, not wanting to walk all the way back to his office.

"This here's Nut Richards, who am I speaking to?"

"Nut, I just thought you might be interested in some information about the sale of the ski area. I understand that you're keen to purchase."

"I might be…who the hell is this?"

"Well, I have some information that there's a local group here in town that's going to try and outbid you. And I have a pretty good idea what they can offer."

"Yeah, so?"

"So if you would be available to pay me something of a finder's fee, I could probably divulge to you a very accurate number as far as what they're gonna bid. If this could help you any."

"Well, hell (wail hail) it sure wouldn't hurt none. What would you be looking for on your end?"

"Well, I run a concert and event promotions company here in town. I'd be looking to handle all your concert booking for the new mountain, you know, that new resort I hear you're planning to build."

"So, tell me your story Mr. ahh…"

"Jack Hammer."

"Mister Jack Hammer."

"Well, these local dirt bags have been raising money all week. It's been in the paper up here. Anyway, I was out last night and heard some drunk dude in a bar, and he said they have raised nine hundred grand for the purchase. So, you know, if that's helpful to you."

"It might be."

"So we'll talk later about me being the head booker for the resort?"

"Yeah, later." Much later. Nut hung up. Then smiled.

***

Danny was numb in disbelief. Everyone was. There had been tears and hugging.

Hamilton just kept shaking his head. "I can't believe this. This might actually do the trick." In his hand he held a cashier's check for half a million dollars.

"Dude, I'm so sorry I didn't bring that by earlier. I just saw the envelope, saw who it was from and didn't think twice about it."

"That's all right, Brian, as long as we have it now."

Pete said, "I still don't get it. It's probably a fake check or something. Where the hell did Framingham get half a million dollars? Last time I saw him last he was living in Tahoe in a Toyota."

Kev said, "I know, seriously. I've seen this guy spend a whole winter living on crackers and ketchup from the Breckenridge condiment stand."

"Yeah, I know," said Brian. "But he sent a note with the check. Apparently he was partying one day at Squaw, and he got talking to this techno geek that was up for the weekend. He was trying to get some start-up off the ground. Something to do with convertible microprocessors."

"So? Framingham doesn't know anything about computers. He barely knows how to work an ATM."

"Yeah, but he could sell shit to a toilet," said Brian. "He went partners with the guy, and the guy was so desperate for a salesman, he gave Framingham thirty percent of any future revenues. Which didn't mean shit at first. Framingham said after one year with this guy his Discover card was maxed out. He was getting paid only in stock, which was worth nothing. But I guess like six months ago they sold the company to AOL. They got some incubator money and then went public. The IPO was five dollars a share, by the end of the day it closed at forty-seven. Framingham was holding over two hundred thousand shares. He's rich. He's like one of these guys you read about in USA Today or something. I called him and asked for a check, and he said sure. I didn't have any idea."

"Well, this is amazing. We might just pull this off," said Jen #1.

"I can't believe it," said Hamilton. Ed just smiled.

***

Danny called Dab to tell him the good news.

"Yeah, it's crazy, remember those guys I told you that picked me up hitchhiking? Right, this guy they used to hang with back in the day, I guess he hit it big out in Silicon Valley. He bailed us out."

"That's awesome Danny, glad to hear. My guys will be happy when they hear it's gonna go through."

"Seems like it. We should have enough to outbid this guy. All we have to do is submit the bid at the auction tomorrow."

"Great man. So, Danny, tell me exactly how this auction is gonna work?"

Chapter Nineteen

Jennings stopped by the Elks for a drink.

"Let me buy you a beer," said Peter Volt, the skinny and severe proprietor.

"You haven't bought me a drink, I don't think…ever. I've been coming here for twenty years."

"I always thought you were…well, you seem a little strange."

"I am."

Volt chuckled. His white western shirt was spotless. His daddy and granddaddy were ranchers.

"I used to hate those long hairs. Called em flag burners. Guess I still don't trust em much. Lotta folks round here feel that way. But if they can pull this off, I think they'd be welcome about any place in town. Lord knows it's been a while since anyone round here felt real prosperous."

"Well, hopefully their bid holds up. Otherwise we're gonna have a damn strip mall explosion."

"Either way, it'll bring in some business. But I'm pulling for them kids. Good luck today." Jennings drained his draft and left two bucks on the bar. He headed over to the hill.

***

The energy in town was buzzing. The auction didn't start until two, but with nothing else to do, they double and triple checked the bank balance and then the Co-Op group headed over before noon.

Hamilton was milling around, chain dipping Copenhagen, a series of brown spittle splashes slowly staining the snow around him as he paced.

Ed and Amy held hands, Danny and Kev looked stoic, Meg beatific. The Tres Hermanas didn't open the shop, but packed bags with burritos to go for the long day ahead. Brian and Pete couldn't take the pressure and went up to make some turns, promising to meet them in time for the bids.

The group walked over towards the hill. People shook their hands. Some people clapped. "Good luck!" Cars tooted their horns. Ed felt goose bumps. A Blazer drove by, a SAVE WINTERLAND flag flapping from

153

its roll bar. They were cautiously optimistic. Framingham's check was their ace in the hole.

They met in front of the Quonset hut. Even with most of the junk and supplies moved out the day before, there wouldn't be much room.

Inside were Hamilton and his attorney, Matt Platte. Joining them were the third party auditor who would run the proceedings, an observer from the bank, and the notary. Degbert pulled up in a flash rental car shortly after one. He took one look at the crowd and removed his tie.

At quarter to two the arbitrator called them to order.

"OK, we have a two hour, open bidding process. This fax machine will act as the only place that legally binding, signature guaranteed bids will be accepted, unless they are hand delivered by an authorized representative. Winterland will accept bids until exactly four pm. Bidders have until that time to continue to bid, or to withdraw their bid. The highest bid at four pm will become the legal owner of Winterland Ski Area, pending certification by the state's attorney general. Any questions?"

"Yeah, does that fax machine even work?" asked Platte. Everyone laughed, even Degbert.

"It hasn't let me down yet," said Hamilton.

Degbert walked outside and called Nut on his Motorola. They'd be in touch every five minutes. Degbert knew all about the leak and was gonna give it his best poker face when the bids rolled. Hopefully he could get them on the first counter. He knew their resources were finite. By every dollar that he kept the deal down his bonus increased. He already had a bottle of Dom chilling on the Richards Oil jet over at the landing field. Soon he hoped to be halfway to Houston, and finally on the way towards his first million.

At two o'clock the auction opened. Nothing happened.

At two seventeen the fax whirred to life. Out came an offer sheet from Nut's development company.

'We have a bid," announced the arbitrator. The secretary got ready to take notes. "The Galveston & Colorado Ski Partners LLC make a cash bid of nine-hundred and ten thousand dollars."

"Duly noted." The secretary wrote down the amount of the bid, and the time, and it was stamped by the notary.

Hamilton couldn't believe it. He was worried about being out bid, and Richards had *dropped* his offer. This might be easier than he thought. Outside, word rippled through the crowd that a bid was in.

"Shit Head just bid," was what was said, and roundly booed. Many of them were shareholders in the nascent company. All of them were in the Co-Op camp.

Hamilton conferred with his counsel. "That's great, let's get our bid in."

"Not so fast. Let's let some time tick off. That way if they try to counter we can play beat the clock," said Platte.

Ed said "he's right, let some time bleed off here Greg. That's fucked up though, the low bid. I guess it wasn't the best kept secret ever, but he knew how much we had as of yesterday, within a thousand dollars. That's not a good sign."

"Thank God for that guy Framingham. Oh man, I can't believe this day is finally here," said Hamilton. "And now it's so stressful."

Ed patted him on the shoulder. "Hang tough, man."

They were able to hold off until three-fifteen.

"Now man."

Platte hand delivered a sheet to the auditor who read it. "The Winterland Ski Co-Op bids one-point one million dollars for Winterland Ski Area."

"Duly noted."

A little cheer went up outside. Degbert went out and made a call. Three minutes later a fax came in.

"The Galveston & Colorado Ski Partners LLC bids one point three million dollars."

"Duly noted."

Hamilton went out for some fresh air, but the crowd edged around him. It was worse out there. People were patting him on the back, practically holding him up. They were handing him dip, but his lip was already packed. Ed put his arm around Greg and spirited him away. Danny asked everyone to give them room. The crowd backed up. They were respectful, but a party atmosphere was prevalent. There was a keg on a ski patrol sled that was keeping sprits light. Jennings was handing out (read: forcing on people) shots of Scotch. Most had heard about the big last minute mystery donor. Speculation as to his identity ranged from a Saudi sheik to Charles Barkley. Jennings told people he suspected it was Soros, but no one seemed to know who that was. The actual golden contributor, Framingham, was currently arguing over a slightly incorrect pizza order with a delivery driver in San Francisco.

3:25. "Let's do it, all the chips on the table, right now!" said Hamilton.

Platte delivered their offer. It was every penny in the newly opened account at First National.

"The Winterland Ski Co-Op bids one million, four-hundred thousand, seven hundred eighteen dollars and twenty three cents."

"Duly noted."

A bigger cheer outside.

"The Co-Op is balling the jack!"

"Bring the noise!"

A pretty girl with braided hair said to her tall and bearded boyfriend "they're all in."

"*We're* all in," he gently corrected her. Responding to her look he added "I sold the Stump Jumper and most of my vinyl to buy a share in the Co-Op." She understood then, more clearly.

3:35. They got another bid. For another cent. Richards was showing his ass. When Ed saw the bid he made a run at Degbert. "You fucking smart ass son of a bitch!" He was restrained and the auditor promptly banned Ed from the proceedings.

Hamilton didn't know what to do. Him and Platte were in huddle outside with Ed and Danny close by.

"Fuck! We'll just—how about we just send Danny over to the bank to make a deposit. I've got like sixty bucks on me," said Hamilton.

"It doesn't matter, man. He'll just re-up his bid. I think they've got you Greg," said Platte. Hamilton looked like he was gonna cry. Jen #2 was crying.

Minutes slipped away.

Hamilton chugged a beer, then another. Ed just kept patting him on the back. "We'll figure this thing out man, I've got a good feeling here."

3:47. The fax whirred to life. Word got out to Hamilton, who went back inside. Danny waited with Ed. "I hope it's not a picture of Nut Richards' balls."

"I hate that fuck."

The arbitrator read the fax. "The Denver Ski Equity LLC bid two million dollars for Winterland Ski Area."

"Duly noted."

Hamilton stumbled outside. "There's another bid."

"What's he trying to do, drive up his own price?"

"No, that's the thing…The bid isn't from Richards."

Ed shook his head. A nervous energy swept the crowd as word of the new bid spread. Danny felt the old calm coming over him.

The bid sent a shock through Degbert. He rushed outside, knocking his chair over.

***

High in the glass tower Nut Richards smashed his fist against the wall.

"God-Damn-It, word's out about the fucking auction! I'm gonna strangle you, you little punk!"

"Don't give me that shit, you wanted a twenty-*four* hour auction."

"We don't have time to argue. Just get us in there."

"Ok, ok, send another offer. We can still make this work, Nut. Get it here. Send it now."

***

A fax came off the old Brother. "The Galveston & Colorado Ski Partners LLC bid two point two million dollars."

"Duly noted."

Ed was stunned. They all were. Whoever was gonna win the bid now, it wasn't gonna be the Co-Op. The crowd started to thin out a little. Some went to catch the last lift of the day, others to drown their sorrows or just see about getting their money back for their now worthless shares.

3:51. Another fax. "The Tahoe Ski Syndicate bids four million dollars for Winterland Ski Area."

"Duly noted."

Degbert turned white. Outside everyone could hear Nut through Degbert's portable phone, screaming from Houston. (You could almost hear him without the phone.) Degbert was talking fast.

"Four million. No, I don't have any idea. Hold one, there's another one coming in, is this us?"

"The Florida Real Estate Trust bid five million dollars."

"Duly noted."

Degbert had never been so confused in his life. Outside the mood had turned bitter. Shadenfreunde ruled. Degbert was jeered, jostled even. Jennings got right in his face.

The Co-Op might be sunk, but the crowd was reveling in watching Nut's stooge take the heat. He was bent at the waist, shouting down the phone in the waning afternoon light.

3:55.

"Degbert, listen to me! You bid five-five and not a penny more. If your projections are accurate, we can still make money. But that's it! When I find the son of bitch who leaked this—the fax is coming right now. Don't let the bidding close."

"The Galveston & Colorado Ski Partners LLC bid five point five million dollars."

"Duly noted."

Degbert couldn't believe it. The faxes kept going. "The New York Legitimate Businessmen Association bid eight million dollars."

"Duly noted."

3:58.

"Did you get the fax?"

"Yeah, but Nut, they just got a bid for eight million and there's still shit coming in."

Nut was quiet for a moment. "Pull the plug. Just get us out." Degbert listened, the speakerphone on Nutt's end transmitted the sounds of shrieking and of furniture smashing. *Aaarrgghh*! It was a high and hollow sound, one that sent chills through Degbert.

3:59.

"The Galveston & Colorado Ski Partners LLC withdraw all previous bids."

"Duly noted."

All the while the fax kept pumping. The arbiter addressed the stunned group. "It looks like we might run out of time here folks, as stated, all faxes must have arrived at or before four pm or they will not be counted."

He grabbed the next fax. "The Dingo Corporation bids twenty million dollars."

"Duly noted."

And then Danny knew what happened.

"The time is now four pm mountain standard time. The auction is closed."

"Duly noted."

Degbert was halfway back to the jet. The Co-Op folks stumbled around outside, shell-shocked, screaming; something was up, they just didn't know what. Danny ran over and gave Jen #2 a big kiss and lifted her up off the ground. She looked stunned. "Don't worry, babe. We did it."

"What?"

***

At a bank of fax machines near the fixed income trading desk at Burnham, Brandt, a group of young men stood smoking cigars.

"I got one! The Ball N Sack corporation!"

"Yeah, send it."

"Fifty million from the Bearded Clam LLC!" Send it! This got a big laugh. Dab called out over the fervor, "All right, all right you guys. Send the call options now. It's after four their time."

***

Pete and Brian were chilling in the shrine. They were nearly comatose. They'd run out of weed around three, but every time they started to leave, people had stopped by and smoked them up. They were helpless.

They looked at each other when they heard the shouting. "We must have won the bid I guess?"

"Far out."

"Thanks Framingham."

"Yeah, to Framingham." They held up the swirled blue and green glass pipe to the west. Wind chimes tinkled in the afternoon breeze. To their guests, "Say, you girls want to go to a party tonight at my buddy Ed's house?"

"Sure."

"Far out."

Reggae music warbled from the old boom box. The sun started to duck behind the peak.

Chapter Twenty

As they wound their way in broken clumps and shifting groups down from the hill and back into town, Danny was hurrying from group to group, telling them that it was gonna be all right. No one knew quite what to think, but Jennings seemed to get it, and Danny's enthusiasm was contagious. He knew Dab had pulled something, but couldn't explain exactly what.

Hamilton looked like he'd been shit on by an elephant.

They'd planned an event at Ed's either way, celebration or eulogy, and now the party was on the upswing. Word flew that the Co-Op had won, despite all the confusion. The whole town showed up. Cars pulled up on the lawn. Ed had four kegs of Fat Tire packed in snow by the deck, and people brought cases of beer and bottles of hooch. Jennings ran up to his place on his motorcycle and returned in a pickup truck with no license plates, its bed packed with snow and bottles of home brew.

Ed got the grill fired up. Of course he believed Danny, but still wasn't sure what had happened. Someone else had the winning bid. By tens of millions of dollars. What difference did it make who? Danny went in the bedroom to call Dab.

***

"Munis, Horowitz."

"Dab, you son of a bitch, what did you do?"

"Oh, I'm sorry, who's calling please? I'm very busy here, having just traded twenty thousand inverse floaters to Merrill Lynch at a two point pop. Plus I'm getting my right shoe shined right now and besides that I'm busy buying a ski area. Oh, and trying to pop a big bag of hot air from Texas."

"Well, you popped it all right, Richards bailed with two minutes to go. His little financial queer took off running."

"Sweet."

"But where are you gonna get twenty million dollars for the Dingo Corporation to buy the hill?"

"That's the Dingo Corporation's problem."

"Does it even exist?"

"Yeah, it exists all right. On paper. It's an S-Corporation that I had set up. My buddy in compliance owed me a favor for getting him laid on Grand Cayman, he did the paperwork for me—what? Yeah, I've got him on the phone right now, as a matter of fact—Hey, yeah, the guys say hi."

"Tell them hi. I still don't know what you did. How will the corporation buy the hill?"

"It won't. I just checked, and the Dingo Corporation, well, let's just say they didn't have a real profitable year last year. Took it up the ass, more like. I don't know who does the books over there, but it turns out they don't actually have any, you know, assets. Wow! Were they ever embarrassed. You can imagine their surprise, right? Same thing with the Miami Ski Concern. And the New York, fuckin', whatever they were. Can you believe the luck? Tough year all over the place. *Those guys* didn't have any money, either."

"So what happens to the bids?"

"Well, after all the bids, we sent call options, essentially retractions. Which, if I understand correctly, should have had tipped the auction to the highest remaining bidder. In other words…"

"…The Co-Op. That's brilliant. But I mean, what if Richards gets suspicious? What if he sues?"

"Oh, I guaran-fucking-tee he sues. And he'll win. But it doesn't matter. He can sue 'til his dick falls off, these corporations are fucked. They have nothing."

"What if he sues you?"

"Sue everybody. It doesn't matter. That's what LLC means, limited liability corporation. Not my problem."

"So even if he does sue, or the attorney general gets wind of it, or whatever, all they can do is go after these paper corporations and not us?"

"Now you're on the trolley. Didn't you take finance sophomore year at Madison?"

"Yeah, but that's when I discovered weed. How'd you know Richards would bail? His offers were real."

"It was risky, Richards could have stayed in the bidding. Not likely, we had a French company called Vulva ready to drop two hundred million dollars if it came to that. I figured he'd drop out at some point. You guys never retracted your bid right?"

"No, we didn't even think to. We got over our heads pretty quick there. You know, some of those retractions came in after four."

"So, sue."

"What if Richards sues the Co-Op?"

"Richards has to prove you or someone at the Co-Op had prior knowledge that these companies were horseshit. Did you have anything to do with sending those bids?"

"No."

"Then you win that suit. Next."

It took a few moments to really marinate.

"You're a fucking evil genius, Dab."

"I do what I can. But let's not forget, I'm a partner in this company now. And I've got some big ideas. They got room on that mountain for a strip club?"

"I gotta get back to the party man, we got some freaked out hippies in the other room. You fucking psychopath."

***

Danny stood on Ed's coffee table and called for quiet. All eyes on him. "I just spoke to my man in Chicago. It was a bag job. We got it. We got the hill."

He was tackled onto the couch and sprayed with beer. Someone cranked the stereo back up. Led Zeppelin IV rocked the house. The party lasted three days.

***

After the party Ed considered moving, but thought it would be slightly easier to clean up. Slightly. It had been wild. Jennings almost died. There was a bonfire. Danny didn't jump in this time.

Hamilton stopped by after a quick shower and two days in bed.

"How you feeling man?"

"Better. You?"

"Well, I don't drink, so the hangover factor isn't there. But the mess..."

"That was some party."

"You're telling me. I've never seen people so wasted. One guy ate two of my forks. It was worth it though. So, the Co-Op takes over, when?"

"June first. Hard to believe, huh?"

"Yeah, you did it, man. What's your first act as president?"

"Stepping down. Well, naming a successor and then stepping down."

"What? Really?"

"Yeah man, I can't take it. I've been to hell and back with this hill. And I love it truly, like I always did. Loved it before it went Co-Op. Loved it before we opened Hinterland. But I just want to ski man. Long as there's some snow, I'll be up there."

"I hear that."

"The Co-Op was your idea. People in town certainly think a lot of you. What do you say? Think you might wanna be president of Winterland Ski Co-Op?"

Amy came from the side yard in a flannel and bandana. She'd been separating broken glass and ripped clothes into piles. She and Ed smiled at each other.

"Yeah, I do believe I'll be hanging around for a while. Yeah man. Sure."

***

The same day the hill closed for the season Turcotte was arrested by the Colorado State Police and charged with police brutality. Jennings won an award for investigative journalism, beating out reporters from papers with circulations tens of thousands, even hundreds of thousands larger than The Wire. At the award presentation he puked on the dais.

Hammer got busted when he sold two grams of cocaine to a twenty-eight year old posing as a high school junior. Tres Hermanas had a record year. The old Trappers location was reopened as an art supply store. Ground was broken on the Winterland Lodge. It was to include shops, ski rentals, restaurants, plus an eighty room ski dormitory where bunks beds cost ten bucks a night. There was to be a brew pub called Easy Ed's.

***

For the first time since he left for football training camp at Carolina, Ed sat in his old man's oak paneled study. He explained how it all went down. How he was gonna be the president, how it was a co-op for the good of the people. He'd done it. He'd made the old man proud. And more importantly, himself.

"So tell me Edward, how was it that you ended up as head of a ski area in Colorado?"

"Well, I was out fishing. It was my last night on the island..."

164

About the Author

Rob Conery is the weekly fishing columnist in the Cape Cod Times. His work has appeared in Cigar Aficionado, Fly Rod & Reel, Powder and The Drake. His short fiction appears in Sand Sports magazine. A graduate of the University of Massachusetts, he splits time between a hobo camp in western Maine and his native Cape Cod, where he has spent 44 consecutive summers walking distance to Lewis Bay. This is his first novel.